GAY ROMANCE COLLECTION VOLUME 4

CONNOR WHITELEY

No part of this book may be reproduced in any form or by any electronic or mechanical means. Including information storage, and retrieval systems, without written permission from the author except for the use of brief quotations in a book review.

This book is NOT legal, professional, medical, financial or any type of official advice.

Any questions about the book, rights licensing, or to contact the author, please email connorwhiteley@connorwhiteley.net

Copyright © 2024 CONNOR WHITELEY

All rights reserved.

DEDICATION
Thank you to all my readers without you I couldn't do what I love.

CLEAN BREAK

CONNOR WHITELEY

No part of this book may be reproduced in any form or by any electronic or mechanical means. Including information storage, and retrieval systems, without written permission from the author except for the use of brief quotations in a book review.

This book is NOT legal, professional, medical, financial or any type of official advice.

Any questions about the book, rights licensing, or to contact the author, please email connorwhiteley@connorwhiteley.net

Copyright © 2024 CONNOR WHITELEY

All rights reserved.

CHAPTER 1
Friday 7th July 2023
Canterbury, England

Harley Cole sat in his best friend's brand-new black Ford something (he never had been good with cars) with the wonderful smell that only brand-new fresh from the factory cars had that reminded him of great sweets as a child, and the soft leather felt so silky against his skin as he sat on the large black passenger seat.

The little black ford drove slowly down the narrow country lanes with thick blackberry bushes lining either side, and Harley actually couldn't remember the last time he had ever been down country lanes. They were just awful in his opinion but his best friend Douglas was just driving so expertly that he didn't mind at all.

Even the delightful hints of blackberry managed to barely cut through the aroma of the new car, Harley realised that he was really going to like this trip.

Granted the dirt country lane road was a little worsen for wear but he didn't mind. These country lanes in the south of England were hardly used too much and every trip with Douglas was a small adventure in its own right.

And as the setting sun turned the sky a striking fiery orange with pink streaks running through it, he realised this was exactly the sort of break him and Douglas needed after finishing up their undergrad degrees.

Harley had loved his psychology degree specialising in clinical psychology, or mental health as he always explained it to everyone, but those last exams were just a nightmare.

Hopefully he passed but he knew he would. He worked way too hard and had barely gone out in the last year to make sure he knew everything he could for those exams.

The little Ford turned left and went down another very long country lane with the blackberry bushes being replaced with tall oak trees with branches shooting out in all directions, managing to block out some of the setting sun.

Birds sang for the final time in the distance before the sun set and Harley just looked at his best friend and was so grateful he had wanted him along.

Harley had to admit that Douglas had to have some sort of ulterior motive because they were currently driving towards Canterbury, England so they could both pay their respects to Douglas's dead grandmother. The entire family was meant to be coming so Harley had no idea why Doug had been so insistent that he came.

Normally Harley would have refused (and he did at first) but Doug had played up the fact that he was so upset and he just wanted a friendly face.

It also didn't exactly help that Harley hadn't been home to Canterbury for the three years of his degree and his parents had always been away on business but they too were back in Canterbury. So it wouldn't exactly be a bad idea to see them in person for once instead of the twice-a-week video chat that normally lasted for an hour or two depending on what him and mum called the "State of The Family" stuff.

He had already agreed to spend all of August with them but he was just looking forward to seeing them.

Harley laughed and he was so excited about seeing his family again and going to the celebrations dedicated to Doug's grandmother.

"Did I ever meet your grandma?" Harley asked.

"Na, I haven't seen her in person for two years. She wrote letters to me and I tried to video chat with her but, she was the enemy of technology,"

Harley just smiled. His nan and grandad were like that.

"You know what's happening this weekend then? And is it possible for me to go and see my parents too?" Harley asked.

"Of course, don't be silly of course. The entire weekend is really free except from the funeral tomorrow morning, the afternoon is dedicated to going around Canterbury and enjoying some of grandma's favourite places and then there's a big family meal tomorrow night,"

From what Harley had heard about Grandma Douglas she was a very funny, crazy woman that loved to have a good time including a lot of dancing, theft and bingo. Harley really hoped he didn't have to play bingo because as much as he knew it wasn't, bingo was just such an old person's game.

"Tonight is just for the out of town lot like us having to travel up from Exeter and my cousin is coming. Have I ever told you about Cousin Jase?"

Harley just shook his head and smiled. That was the reason why Doug had invited him here but the last he heard of Jase he was with a boyfriend of five years, they were happy, cute and very hot together.

"Him and his boyfriend broke up last month. It's a shame because the guy was hot and without Jase I wouldn't have realised I was gay until I went to uni,"

Harley just nodded. This was a setup plain and simple but of course, Harley *may* have seen Jase on Doug's social media a few times and he had to admit Jase was hot as hell, but he was far cuter than his boyfriend.

As the immense cathedral spire of Canterbury came into view, Harley just smiled and sat back in the wonderful little Ford and waited for them to arrive.

He had a little feeling that this weekend was going to be extremely fun, attractive and really worthwhile. And that was hardly a bad thing.

CHAPTER 2
Friday 7th July 2023
Canterbury, England

When Jase Craycraft went into the lobby of the little hotel he had booked away from the family in the centre of Canterbury, he was so glad he knew about this perfect little hidden gem of a place. The lobby was perfectly built with its small polished wooden walls that had paintings, articles and photos of Canterbury through the centuries. It was such a perfectly stunning city with so many secrets that Jase loved.

The thick blue carpet felt so springy under his black shoes and the smell of lavender, jasmine and honey was so delightful that Jase knew that he was going to have a great weekend here. It was going to be brilliant because he was finally having a chance to see his family again after studying away for so long but if things got a little too much for him then he could simply come back to this paradise of a small hotel and get some peace and quiet.

Jase went over to the small wooden reception desk that was currently empty but at least the huge computer was still on so someone had to be about, there were accounts opened on the desk and the little brass lamp lighting them up flickered a few times.

It clearly had seen better days but Jase really didn't mind. This place was nice, cheap and it was a safe heaven away from the family. Especially as they would all be asking what happened between him and his boyfriend.

And Jase really didn't want to have to go through the very awkward excuses of that he didn't know what happened between them. They had met in the last year of sixth form when they were 17, they had both got to the same university and still loved each other and then they got a wonderful flat together for the Masters and then they both just realised they didn't love each other anymore.

And it wasn't like they hadn't tried everything first. They had tried to go out for dinner more often, they did their favourite thing together like bowling, hikes and more and they even tried couples therapy using a friend of Jase's that wanted some experience.

None of it worked and Jase couldn't blame his boyfriend. Michael was hot, young and just flat out beautiful but maybe he was right when he said that him and Jase just weren't made for relationships yet.

Jase flat out disagreed because all he wanted in the entire world was a boyfriend he could love, treasure and just get to know.

"Hello Jase darling, how are you?" a very tall woman asked with a beehive hairstyle as she got behind the desk.

"Good thanks. Is my room ready?"

"Sure is dear," the woman said, "and is Mr Douglas Craycraft a relative of yours? It's a weird surname and I didn't know if you wanted their room near or far away from you?"

Jase laughed. It was flat out wonderful that his slightly younger cousin was also coming here. He had to admit that Douglas had to be his favourite family member after his parents, of course, Douglas was great, fun and with him being the only other gay in the family he was a great person to talk to about boy issues.

"It's your choice. I would prefer them to have a room close to me but I don't want to put you out," Jase said.

"Don't be silly dear. You are my favourite customer and you must come down here more often," she said. "I'll give them the room next to you,"

Jase nodded his thanks. At least he could talk to Douglas about things that weren't sport, straight sex or the hottest female celebrities like the rest of his brothers would want to talk about.

And as much as Jase didn't want to admit it, he was really excited about this weekend. He got to see his great family, have fun and have a dinner honouring the very special Grandma Craycraft.

Jase still didn't know too much about her but it was grandma that made him feel safe enough to come out and he was so glad that he did. He owned his entire life to grandma Craycraft so he wasn't going to miss this for the entire world.

"Jase!" someone shouted behind him.

Jase turned around and suddenly found himself being hugged by Douglas who looked great in his blue skin-tight jeans, white crisp shirt and black trainers (they were so much easier to drive in than shoes).

Pure delight filled Jase, he was so looking forward to catching up with Douglas and learning everything about him over the past few years and-

Wow, just wow.

Jase hadn't noticed the hottie walking in behind Douglas with his fit-as-fuck body without a shred of fat on his tall, lean frame. And Jase absolutely loved his board shoulders, skinny legs and his perfectly handsome face. Jase had no idea who the hell he was but he loved how the hottie's brown hair was seductively styled parted to the right.

His wonderful hair looked so soft, seductive and long that all Jase wanted to do was run his fingers and kiss the man's hot sexy lips that just looked so damn full and soft.

Then he realised that if a hot man was coming with Douglas then it was probably his boyfriend.

Damn Jase just kept focusing on how hot the

man was and it was going to be a painfully long weekend if that hottie really was Douglas's boyfriend.

It was just a shame the hot boys were always taken.

CHAPTER 3
Friday 7th July 2023
Canterbury, England

Harley was just flat out amazed at the sheer hunk of a man standing in front of him. Sure, on social media, he had seen plenty of hot pictures of Jase in crop tops, large vests and more than showed just how muscular and amazingly fit his body was, but actually seeing him in person was something else.

Jase might have been wearing a loose plain grey t-shirt but Harley could still see just how fit he was with a six-pack and very nicely sculptured shoulders and biceps. Jase was just so perfectly stunning that Harley really didn't know what to do.

He had met Greek god-like boys before and that had always gone badly. He normally ended up saying something stupid, acting weird and just getting laughed at. But considering how he was stuck here for the entire weekend and now they were staying at the same hotel there was no chance of escaping Jase, he really couldn't afford that.

Harley felt the sweat pour down his back. His heart pounded in his chest. He really wanted to run away but his legs weren't working.

Harley forced himself to take a nice refreshing breath of the flora scented air that was a little too strong for him and he forced his mouth to work.

"Hi I'm Harley and single," Harley said.

Harley gasped as the stupid words fell out of his mouth and he just covered his mouth with his hands. He so badly wanted the ground to swallow him whole.

He actually felt a little sick and he went lightheaded. He had met hot men before but he didn't know why he was having such a strong reaction to this hunk of a man. Normally he at least tried to play it a little cooler and now he understood why he was single.

Doug hugged him slightly and Harley still couldn't take his eyes off the hottie in front of him. Jase was just so hot with his body and from what Doug mentioned Jase was a graduate like them but he hadn't mentioned the subject.

"That's great to hear, I thought you were Douglas's boyfriend," Jase said.

Harley had no idea why Jase was happy he was single. Was there interest? Was there a chance?

Harley forced himself to calm down, Jase might have been seriously hot but he had to focus on being there for his best friend this weekend. This was going to be a tough time for the entire family and the last thing he wanted was for Doug to be blamed for bringing a horny idiot to a family event.

He just couldn't embarrass Doug like that.

"Hey Jase, I hear the others are going into the city centre tonight to grab some dinner before the rest of the horde arrives tomorrow. Want to join?" Doug asked.

Harley just looked at his best friend. He knew that the Craycraft family was a fairly massive group but calling them a horde made it sound like they were vast.

"How many coming tonight?" Jase asked.

"Twenty-five," Doug said. "Mainly the cousins and the international lot,"

Harley really couldn't believe what he was hearing. In his family they were lucky to have twenty-five people in the entire family let alone a small portion of it, before the real horde came tomorrow.

"How many coming tomorrow?" Harley asked.

Doug laughed. "I don't know. Maybe a hundred or more that's just the British lot. We sent invites to over two hundred of Grandma's friends,"

Harley just shook his head. He normally hated crowds with a passion but he was really looking forward to it and as Doug got them checked in, all Harley could do was focus on sexy Jase and he noticed that Jase looking at him too.

As much as Harley wanted there to be a connection between them, he knew he was probably just making stuff up. He had done it before by falling for straight guys who he believed were sending him signals so he couldn't allow that to happen again.

He had to focus on being the greatest of friends he could to Doug instead of focusing on an insanely hot man he probably didn't have a chance with.

But as Doug came over and all three of them took their suitcases up to their rooms to get settled in before they went to dinner, Harley had to admit he was just a little excited about their room being next to Jase.

Maybe it was random, maybe it was a sign of attraction, or maybe it was just a sign of what was going to happen later.

And that little idea excited him a lot more than he ever wanted to admit.

CHAPTER 4
Friday 7th July 2023
Canterbury, England

Jase still couldn't believe how much of a nervous wreck he had been as he showered, changed into a nice shirt and then showered again because he was sweating so much at the very idea of seeing beautiful Harley again. He knew that it was silly and it was beyond strange because he had never ever had this sort of reaction to a man before, but at least they were now at the restaurant.

Jase had always loved how weird Canterbury was with its little cafes, restaurants and other delights down every single street that shot out of the main high street that basically acted like a spine for the beautiful historical city.

Him, Harley and Douglas had all gotten into a very old wooden building dating back from the Victorian era to meet up with the sheer numbers of the family. And it certainly wasn't as nice as the places in Bath but it was cosy enough to make him comfortable.

And he was seeing his family so he hardly minded.

The dark wooden beams of the restaurant were nice and thick, a crackling fire was roaring away in the middle with huge nobly tables around it. There were tons of people of different weights, classes and ages in the restaurant so it had to be good.

Thankfully the staff had pulled together about ten tables for the entire family to come around. There were already all the aunts, cousins and uncles around the table laughing and smiling away.

The smiles only grew as the three of them went over and they all hugged each other. It was so good to see Aunt Beatrice wearing her massive blue dress that she just somehow managed to pull off and Uncle Peterson in his fishing gear. He was always fishing and always had crazy stories to tell.

Jase damn well loved this family.

As they were slightly late because of Jase having to take a second shower and debating about having a third (he was still sweating even now), there was only the small table with three seats left at the end.

Douglas made sure to take the single seat, which Jase was fairly sure he did on purpose the criminal, so Jase had to sit next to Harley who smelt sensational with his earthy aftershave and his amazingly fit body was really highlighted in his fresh crispy light blue shirt.

He was beautiful.

As Jase took his seat he felt his heart pound in his chest as he realised he was actually going to be spending a lot of time with Harley over the weekend, and he didn't mind that idea at all.

The young waitress wearing a black uniform, red tie and a worn notebook smiled at them as she took their drinks and whilst Douglas spoke to the relatives Jase smiled at Harley.

"So Doug tells me you studied a clinical psych Masters in Bath. What was that like?" Harley asked.

Jase's smile grew even more. "It was great. Getting to learn about mental health, theories and getting practical experience at a local clinic. That was brilliant and Bath is a wonderful city that I am really looking forward to returning too in September,"

"You doing your DClinPsych?"

Jase was actually really impressed. Not a lot of people knew what a Doctorate of Clinical Psychology was, let alone that it was something that he had to do if he wanted to become a doctor working with patients with mental health conditions.

He knew that Harley was clever but he knew exactly what he wanted out of life and most importantly what he had to do to get there.

"Yeah, I start in September and then four years later after a lot of experience and research I will be Doctor Craycraft,"

"Very nice,"

Jase had to admit that Harley had such a

beautiful smile that really did light up the fairly dark restaurant, but he also realised that they might have been attracted to each other (that was a massive *might*) but they could never act on anything because they could never be together.

Unless Harley was doing his Masters or whatever he was doing next in Bath or he supposed if Harley was staying at Exeter then it would have been easy for them to see each other, but the problem was it was July so he would have already accepted a place somewhere.

"So what are you doing in September? A year in work? Masters? What?" Jase asked.

Harley laughed and Jase bit his lip as he realised he seriously couldn't have sounded any more desperate and it wouldn't have been hard for Harley to guess why he was asking.

Damn it. All Jase wanted was to act cool, calm and professional, and for some reason Harley was making that flat out impossible.

The young waitress returned with two diet cokes and Jase thanked her.

"I'm coming home for my Masters in clinical psych. I'm studying at Kent University,"

Jase forced himself to smile and he realised that even if they started something here, it could only ever be for a weekend because in September they would have to go back to their lives at opposite ends of the country, and like all long-distance relationships theirs would fail.

The thought of that just killed Jase.

CONNOR WHITELEY

CHAPTER 5
Friday 7th July 2023
Canterbury, England

Harley flat out couldn't believe just how much fun he was having talking to Jase. They had spoken constantly about psychology, the best models for mental health treatment (and agreed to disagree in their minor argument) and he had just loved every single moment with Jase.

He had just never met someone as engaging, interesting and clever as Jase before. Sure Douglas was amazing in his own way but he did a computer science degree, and as much as they talked to each other about what they were learning the conversations just weren't the same.

Even the restaurant wasn't too bad considering it was in one of the isolated little roads off the high street that seriously no one went down normally because it was the type of street that screamed mugging.

But Harley rather liked the rough white walls, the thick black beams and the roaring fire. Yet it was the amazing food that Harley loved, his crispy chilli chicken was just out of this world for his starter and his juicy, crispy sticky ribs for his main was the best he had ever had.

As soon as he got back to the hotel, he was so leaving a review on all the tourist websites because people really needed to come here, and it was just a little thing he could do to help the restaurant.

"I'll be back in a moment," Jase said.

Harley just stared at Jase's great ass as he walked away from the table with a small group of relatives who were going out for a smoke. Jase didn't smoke but he looked to be enjoying the time with his family.

Harley still couldn't believe just how much he was enjoying himself. He actually felt guilty about feeling this great, happy and revitalised considering everyone was here for the funeral tomorrow. He sort of felt like he was dishonouring his best friend's family by enjoying himself too much.

"So?" Doug said leaning over the table. "He's hot isn't he? You two should so go out,"

Harley laughed and shook his head. "This is a funeral weekend. I can't ask a guy out no matter how much I like him,"

"I knew it!" Doug said a lot louder than he probably knew to as he punched the air. "I knew it. I am such a matchmaker and you can tell how much he likes you,"

Harley felt his stomach fill with butterflies. "Really? You think so?"

Doug laughed. "Seriously? You're a uni grad and you still don't know when a guy is hitting on you and likes you?"

Harley playfully hit Doug round the head. "I'm being respectful to your family during this most difficult of times,"

Both of them laughed as they noticed that no one, absolutely no one around the tables were crying, sad or even talking about Grandma Craycraft and to be honest Harley sort of felt like Grandma would have liked that.

"Just ask him out, have fun and just relax. I know you almost burnt out this year at uni so please mate, just have some fun," Doug said.

"Thanks Doug,"

"Douggy darling," a very short cousin said as she came over to the table and Doug went off to talk to her.

Harley had no idea who she was exactly but Doug had made a very good point, and he actually did burnt out badly one night to the point that he had made himself ill and sick. Harley knew that Doug was already concerned about him as it was so he didn't dare tell him what happened.

But Doug was definitely right. He needed to enjoy himself, have fun and just relax for this weekend and for the whole summer if he was being really honest with himself.

And he actually couldn't think of anything more fun than spending it with such a beautiful, perfect, clever man as Jase.

Jase came back over to the table frowning a little. "This is my sister and she's staying in my room,"

Harley forced himself to smile and shake the cousin's hand because both him and Jase had a new problem. Each of their hotel rooms only had spare room for two people and now both rooms were filled.

They weren't getting any private time this weekend that was for sure and Harley really didn't like that idea.

Not for a single moment.

CHAPTER 6
Friday 7th July 2023
Canterbury, England

As Jase went down the long hotel corridor with the wonderfully soft blue carpet under his shoes, the sweet aroma of flowers filling his senses and Harley walking next to him with his sister Fanny and Douglas walking behind them, he just couldn't believe she had actually come.

Jase really, really loved his amazing sister because she was always fun, excited and always had stories to tell from her international banking job but she hadn't said she was coming here. And she certainly hadn't mentioned she was staying with him.

All Jase had wanted tonight was to suggest to handsome Harley to come back into his room for a very innocent nightcap that might lead to more, but that was never going to happen now.

Especially as the very last thing he would ever want for poor Harley was to be interrogated by

Fanny. She was a brilliant banker and negotiator but she was a Pitbull when it came to his boyfriends. Even Michael had failed the test first of all and they had almost broken up years ago because of it.

All of them got to their large blue doors of their hotel rooms, Fanny said goodnight and went straight in and Douglas did the same.

So it was only him and the most handsome man he had ever seen left in the corridor, and he could have sworn the air was cracking with sexual tension, affection and attraction between them. All Jase wanted to do in that moment was kiss the perfect man he was so interested in.

But he couldn't, he just couldn't not with his sister in the next room.

Harley moved closer to him and Jase went closer to him just out of instinct and sheer lust.

Jase loved the feeling of Harley's warm, wonderful breath on his lips and as their lips grazed-

"Jase! I forget my toothbrush can I use yours please?" Fanny shouted.

Jase just laughed and moved away. That was a hell of a mood killer and he just wanted to hug Harley.

"I'll see you tomorrow and thank you, thank you for tonight. I really enjoyed it," Harley said.

"Thank you too," Jase said before they both just disappeared into their hotel rooms.

The entire hotel room was just a large box room with sterile white walls, more wonderfully soft blue carpet and a double bed that was now covered in all of Fanny's stuff from her small suitcase. He had no idea whatsoever how the hell one woman could fit so much, rubbish in a single suitcase.

He could have sworn it was a superpower of women.

The bed had two little wooden bedside cabinets and he was looking forward to reading from his tablet. There were new academic papers just released today on some depression treatments that he wanted to read, but as Fanny started singing off the little en-suite he doubted he was going to be able to concentrate.

"Harley's hot. Is he straight or Douglas's boyfriend?" Fanny asked from the en-suite.

Jase smiled because he actually felt better now about thinking it himself, at least he wasn't the only one that read that little thing completely wrong.

"Not his boyfriend, just best friend," Jase said as he went over to the bed and moved a large pile of bras so he could sit down.

"How long you staying?" Jase asked.

Then he heard Fanny just stop moving about in the en-suite and Jase sat up perfectly straight as he realised that something was wrong. His sister was many things but she wasn't one to sit still under any circumstances.

Slowly the bright white en-suite door opened and Fanny came out, shut the door and leant against it.

"For a few weeks and then I'm off to Australia to

lead a new team at the local branch of the bank,"

"That's brilliant, you've always wanted to travel to Oceania," Jase said.

Fanny nodded and smiled but Jase had spent their teenage years together and his sister was the first person to know he was gay. He knew when she was forcing her face to look a certain way.

"What's wrong?"

"Jase, I want to come home. I love travelling, don't get me wrong but I'm five years older than you, pushing 30 and I have never had a serious relationship. Always moving place to place, I don't want that life anymore,"

Jase just went over to her and hugged her tight. "I would love nothing more than having my big sister home,"

They both laughed as Jase was so glad to hear that and it was only now he was realising just how close they were and how much he missed her.

"Now," Fanny said looking him dead in the eye. "Tell me what's going on between you and Harley?"

Jase just smiled because the Pitbull was back and he really did love his sister.

CHAPTER 7
Saturday 8th July 2023
Canterbury, England

As Harley laid in the large single bed just staring up at the ceiling in the pitch darkness and the gentle snoring of Doug kept him company, he had to admit that he really, really liked Jase. There was just something so special about him, he was kind, caring and just so hot.

Harley had hated it when they had to break their almost-kiss. He didn't know what had actually come over him because he never planned to kiss him but he was so glad he almost did.

And all Harley wanted more than anything in the world was to make that kiss more than an almost-kiss. He seriously wanted to kiss Jase's big soft lips and just treasure the taste, feeling and tenderness.

But as Doug snored louder and louder he realised that flat out wasn't going to happen, and he was going to have to watch a hot man from far away over the course of the weekend, and he really didn't like that idea very much. He liked Jase so there just had to be a way to get a few moments with him.

Harley rolled over and simply allowed the heavenly softness of the great bed to claim him, he had to make sure that he got alone time with the man he was seriously falling over. So he was going to have to be more proactive and he had to *make* this happen.

The almost-kiss had told him all he needed to know about Jase's feelings towards him. They both wanted, needed, longed for this but they needed someone to make the first move.

And that person had to be Harley.

Something banged.

Water poured onto Harley's fast.

He screamed.

He shot off the bed.

Harley went over to the lights and just gasped when he saw that a busted water pipe had exploded over his single bed and it was now flooded.

More pipes banged.

Chunks of ceiling collapsed.

The entire room flooded.

Doug jumped up.

Harley grabbed him.

Running out of the hotel room.

Harley was so glad he was basically fully clothed as Doug came out in just his black tight boxers, and Harley definitely wasn't ashamed when he wondered if Jase wore similar stuff. If so then he was so looking forward to having adult fun with him.

"What's going on?" the hotel owner said with the beehive hair style as she marched up the corridor.

"Our room's flooded," Harley said.

"Oh, damn it. I paid those cowboys to fix my water pipes a decade ago and they promised it would last until I died," the woman said, coughing and even from this distance Harley could smell how much she smoked.

Maybe the cowboy builders didn't think she had that long left to live.

"You know, damn it, you know I will call my daughter at the Heaven Canterbury she'll get you a new room," the woman said.

Harley was about to protest for some reason that he actually didn't know but the woman waved him silent and got out her phone.

Doug started shivering and he was soaking wet, and Harley just wished Jase was in Doug's place instead. There was nothing he wanted more than to simply hug a wet, soaking Jase who needed a little warming up.

Harley tried to shake the idea away. He normally wasn't this horny, uncontrolled and sexual. He was normally so calm, collected and he just waited for boys to hit on him.

Harley had no idea whatsoever why he was thinking so much about Jase, minus the fact he was so hot, of course.

"What's going on?" Jase asked as him and Fanny

came out of their room and Fanny immediately went over to Doug and placed her dressing gown over him.

Harley laughed as Doug looked a little silly in a bright pink dressing gown but at least Doug was warm now and he wasn't going to catch a cold or anything.

Doug told Jase and Fanny what had happened and Harley was a little curious about why Jase was smiling so much. Harley and Doug had lost most of their stuff and it was going to take ages to dry everything.

"That is just sensational," the woman said. "My daughter says there is a spare room at the Heaven Canterbury for you to enjoy. I'll call the insurance company in the morning and we'll see about replacing your stuff,"

"Your insurance company is open on a weekend?" Harley asked.

"I don't pay premium for no benefits," the woman said laughing.

Harley shrugged that was a fair point but he did want to be a little more proactive about beautiful Jase.

But Doug stepped forward. "Actually Fanny, I haven't seen you for ages. Let's catch up and we can share the room whilst these two… share,"

Harley couldn't believe how the owner of the hotel laughed and nodded, Fanny did the same and Doug basically gently pulled Fanny towards the reception desk.

"I was going to say the same thing," Harley said.

Jase laughed. "We haven't exactly got much of an option now,"

Harley just grinned like a little schoolboy as he went into Jase's hotel room and his entire body was shaking.

He had no idea what was about to happen.

CHAPTER 8
Saturday 8th July 2023
Canterbury, England

What the hell was happening?

Jase had absolutely no idea what to do as he led beautiful, sexy, handsome Harley into his hotel room. It was a mess and Fanny's things still covered every single inch of the place. It was a nightmare.

Jase gasped as he noticed that pink underwear, makeup and basically every thing a drag queen needed. It wasn't that Jase was against them in the slightest, he had plenty of drag friends back in Bath that were wonderful guys but he didn't want Harley to get the wrong impression of him.

"I take it Fanny doesn't travel light?" Harley asked.

Jase gently fell against a cold white wall of the hotel room as he heard wonderful Harley say that. He was relieved that Harley knew this stuff wasn't his and that he wasn't someone different than the guy Harley had known all night.

He felt his stomach churn and tighten and flip into a painful knot as he realised there was only one night. Him and Fanny had sort of created a pillow wall down the centre because apparently he moved a lot in the night.

He didn't believe Fanny.

But he seriously didn't want to do that with handsome Harley, it just seemed so wrong but it also seemed wrong to just sleep with the beautiful man after only knowing him for a few hours.

Harley folded his arms and looked just as panicked about the bed situation.

"Let's just make our feelings known and let's see how this works," Jase said.

Harley nodded and Jase was so excited about this now and all the tension that had built in his shoulders and chest and arms had melted away.

"I really like you Harley. I think you're cute, clever and really fun to be around. And if you don't mind, I would like to, sleep with you tonight,"

Jase really wasn't a fan of how strained some of the words sounded but liked Harley way too much to risk him running away.

Harley grinned and took a step closer. "I really like you too. You're really fit, really smart and I would love to sleep with you tonight,"

Jase bit his lower lip for a moment. "Just sleep,"

Harley laughed and came over to him and Jase loved feeling his skinny arms wrap around his waist.

And blood rushed to his wayward parts, so Jase wrapped his own strong muscular arms around Harley.

It was so cute when Harley gasped in pleasure.

"Yes, only sleep tonight. I, I don't want to get too involved because of what happens after this weekend,"

Jase forced himself to weakly smile as he pulled Harley close and the handsome man he was falling for buried his face in Jase's shoulder. Jase really didn't like what Harley had said but it was true.

Anything they did together would only last a single weekend, so it was sort of best to keep each other at some distance so the heartbreak might be slightly better after this weekend.

But Jase knew it was a simple lie that he admitted was a good one, and yet it was so flawed. If the two of them didn't fall in love (Jase already had partly), make love and just make the most of this weekend then he knew he was going to regret it for the rest of his life.

And he just knew, really knew that Harley was going to feel the exact same way.

Jase raised Harley's head with a finger and just stared into those deep striking eyes that were almost as beautiful as the rest of the handsome man.

"We'll figure it out," Jase said, "but I just want to enjoy you tonight,"

Jase kissed him and he moaned in pleasure as the softness, tenderness and sheer taste of Harley's wonderful lips were better than he ever could have imagined. It was easily a million times better than other kisses he had had.

Harley pushed Jase over to the bed and Jase just knew this was going to be an amazing night for sure.

CHAPTER 9
Saturday 8th July 2023
Canterbury, England

Harley had really loved last night. It had been a magical, hot, sweaty night of passionate love and the best sex he had ever had before. He had no idea a man could do even a quarter of those things before last night and as much as he loved it, Harley seriously didn't want last night to end, let alone this weekend.

Harley laid right next to Jase in their bed and he just listened to the wonderful heartbeat of the man he was deeply falling for. And he gently ran his fingers down Jase's rock-hard body.

He was really impressed that Jase's chest was perfectly sculptured in a nice subtle way and he had such a great thin waist that was seductively average but Harley really loved Jase's washboard abs.

Harley had no idea whatsoever what it was about *Jase's* body that he loved so much because he had had plenty of great sex with gym boys before, but Jase was just so wonderfully different. It was probably all because *he* was a great person as well.

The warm gentle snoring of Jase was so much better than Doug's and he was glad to have such a great friend that loved and cared about him. It seemed Doug wanted him and Jase to make it work no matter what, but could that actually happen?

Harley wanted it to, but even if they were together for the summer, Jase would still be moving back to Bath on the opposite end of England for four years and DClinPsychs weren't exactly known for great social hours because it was so much work, fun work granted but work nonetheless.

And Harley would still be in Canterbury working on a Masters that he was so excited about. He loved clinical psychology and he wouldn't change it for the entire world.

They were stuck.

"What's the time?" Jase asked as he kissed Harley.

Harley had to admit that each kiss was getting better and better and if kisses had the power to make someone into a messy puddle of pleasure then he was fairly sure he would have been melted hours ago.

"We have about two hours before we need to be at the funeral," Harley said.

Jase grinned and pulled Harley against him. "Great, want to go for round two?"

Harley laughed. "I would love to but I need real breakfast and I want to be there for Doug today,"

"Good point. How's he doing? Him and grandma were so close when they were younger,"

Harley rolled over so he was facing handsome Jase. "He's doing okay but I think he's distracting himself by making sure us two get together,"

Jase laughed. "Well I'm glad he did and I'm really glad it's working,"

Harley kissed the beautiful man he was falling for so quickly and really, really wanted Jase never to leave Canterbury. And if he could change his Masters Harley actually would because he believed they both had a real shot at making this work.

But that was the problem with university places, once you accepted them you didn't dare let them go in case you couldn't find another one.

And Harley really doubted Bath had any spare places anyway.

In a moment of madness Harley had actually applied to Bath but they hadn't even had the decency to send him a rejection letter, or these days, email.

Harley kissed Jase a few more wonderful times as a sorry and Jase started kissing Harley's neck as he looked at his phone.

Harley was a little surprised that Doug had tried to call him a few times so he phoned him back and forced himself not to laugh as Jase tried to subtly tickle him. He was seriously starting to fall for sexy Jase.

"Hi mate," Doug said, "can you get to the funeral early please? It's your parents are here and they want to see you,"

Harley just gasped. He had completely forgotten that he wanted to surprise his parents with a visit, he had said he was going to stay with them for a month in August but he wanted to be extra nice.

How had his parents found out he was here now?

"Mate?" Doug asked.

"Um yeah. I'm here. I'll be there as soon as I can, is everything okay?"

"Of course they just want to see you," Doug said.

But as Harley hung up the phone he sort of had a little feeling that Doug wasn't telling him something, because his parents had been great friends with Grandma Craycraft but they normally hated funerals.

So why had they come now and what would they think of Jase when they met him?

The answer to those two questions scared Harley a lot more than he ever wanted to admit.

CHAPTER 10
Saturday 8th July 2023
Canterbury, England

Something Jase really hadn't missed in the past few years was the awfully famous Canterbury traffic, and he really believed that the real definition of a city was the badness of the traffic. In a normal town or village a short drive should have taken a person an average of ten minutes, but in a city a short drive would easily take a poor soul half an hour at a minimum.

That was the real definition of a city.

Taking the hour long drive to just travel a single mile across canterbury, Jase loved holding Harley's wonderfully soft hand as they both went to the funeral that was the strangest location Jase had ever seen.

Grandma Craycraft wanted to have her funeral in a massive lustrous green field on the side of a large hill. Now that sort of made perfect sense because at least she could have all of her family, friends and every other Tom, Dick and Harry at her service, but it was even more of a pain than normal because of the bad traffic.

Jase actually felt sorry for the poor souls that had to drive from central Canterbury at the hotel Heaven Canterbury like Douglas.

As Jase moved his hand so he wrapped his arm around Harley's wonderfully thin waist, the field was actually rather perfect. The grass was thick, green and full of life and even the endless rows of handcrafted wooden benches seemed to fit so perfectly in this field.

The day was bright, sun but it was great that it wasn't too hot so there was no chance of people sweating. That was a god send considering they would need all the moisture their bodies could get for crying, and Jase really liked the sweet aroma of roses, lavender and oranges that clung to the air.

They were also Grandma Craycraft's favourite scents. This really was a perfect funeral for her.

There were tons of people already here in black dresses, suits and jeans. Jase wasn't sure if Grandma Craycraft would approve of the black because she hated funerals for that reason and with black absorbing heat, it was hardly practical for a hot summer day.

Jase kept leading Harley up towards the front of the service were the family was sitting, like Jase's and Douglas's parents and he was just looking forward to seeing them again.

Hopefully Douglas would be okay and he knew that was why Harley was being so quiet. They were both concerned about a lot of things like the funeral, their relationship and how it was probably going to fail after this weekend. But Jase refused to think about it.

He was just going to enjoy every single moment he had with this beautiful stunning man.

"Doug," Jase said as he waved his best friend over.

Jase just grinned at Douglas as he came over to them grinning like he was some kind of evil mastermind that was the cupid of their relationship.

"Good night last night?" Douglas asked, knowing exactly what happened.

"Very good," Jase said really wanting to kiss Harley but they were at a funeral after all.

"Where my parents?" Harley asked.

Doug looked around and waved at something behind them and Jase got the sense that he was about to meet his future in-laws. His stomach churned at the very idea.

When he had met Michael's parents, it had been at a wonderful restaurant in Bath, the garlic snails had been delightful, the French atmosphere so romantic and his parents had been real delights, even after him and Michael broke up it had been his parents that had texted Jase daily to make sure he was okay for the first week. That was exactly how great they were.

Jase really wanted to meet Harley's parents in a similar way. Maybe take them to the Café Rogue in the high street, maybe meet them for coffee or even offer to cook them a Sunday dinner like real families did.

But nope, he was going to have to meet them at a funeral and it was probably going to come to light that he had sex with their son only a few hours after they met. And in his experience, Jase just knew that never went down well.

This was going to be the worse funeral of his little life.

Jase turned around and was really surprised as a very tall, elegant and rather dazzling woman in her late forties came towards them. He was seriously impressed with her bright yellow dress that she somehow managed to pull off, her 6-inch heels and her little pink sparkling handbag looked great too.

Now that was exactly the sort of funeral outfit Grandma Craycraft would have loved.

Then next to her was a very attractive man also in his late forties wearing a red chequered shirt, blue jeans and hiking boots. Again another very good funeral outfit.

"You two look great. Grandma Craycraft would have loved seeing you," Jase said before he could stop himself.

Harley, his parents and Douglas laughed, Jase almost felt a little embarrassed so he hugged Harley even tighter.

"So this is charming psych grad that our son fell for in the space of a few hours," Harley's mother said. "Dougy has told us so much about you,"

"All good I hope,"

The mother shrugged and the father laughed slightly. Jase really wanted to know exactly what Douglas had told them but the parents were still standing there and they hadn't told their son to get away from him so Jase was taking that as a little win at least.

"He is a looker," the mother said. "Oh my, I'm so sorry Jase. I am Penny Cole, Harley's mum, and this is my amazing husband Thomas Cole,"

Jase shook both their hands very hard. It was always best to try and make himself seem as manly as possible when first meeting parents, and a good hard firm handshake was always the best way to do that.

"I trust my son was good last night," Thomas said more of a statement than a question.

Jase just looked at Thomas, he wasn't answering that question, but after a moment everyone laughed.

"Relax Jase, my dad likes embarrassing people," Harley said.

"What? Me? I don't like embarrassing people but you know how we found out Har was gay. We caught him one evening kissing the neighbour kid in his bedroom when we were hosting a massive party,"

Jase looked at the beautiful man he was really falling for and he realised that Harley was trying to frown and smile at the same time. Clearly the boy he was kissing was wrapped up in a lot of good and bad memories that he didn't want his father reminding him about.

Jase noticed how everyone was basically seated now at the funeral so he gestured they should all get to the front and take their own seats.

"Doug said something was wrong on the phone," Harley said.

"Oh Dougy, I told you not to alarm him. there's nothing wrong sweetheart, it's just that we're glad you're coming down next year and I was wondering if you wanted to get a dog with us in August,"

Jase had to admit that was probably the strangest thing he had heard in a while, but it did also make sense. From what Harley had told him about his parents, they did work a hell a lot so it would be impossible to have a dog with them both working full time but if Harley was living at home then it would be easier.

"I would love that!" Harley shouted.

Jase laughed and Harley was just so damn cute but it also meant it was yet another reason for him to stay in Canterbury and not come to see him in Bath.

That was another strike against their relationship and that was really starting to concern Jase a lot more than he ever wanted to admit.

CHAPTER 11
Saturday 8th July 2023
Canterbury, England

Harley had to admit that before today he really hadn't liked funerals but thankfully Grandma Craycraft was way too intelligent to have a traditional funeral that was all about God and not about her. It really made perfect sense because a lot of her friends were Hindus, atheists and basically not a single one of her friends or family were Christians in the slightest so a religious funeral made no sense.

Harley's mouth actually hurt from laughing so much, there were so many great stories about Grandma Craycraft that he was almost upset that he never had such a great chance to meet her.

She really did sound like a wonderful woman.

All the children, grandchildren and other important members of the funeral had all gotten up and said something about their grandma, mother or best friend.

Harley hugged beautiful Jase tight after his speech because it had been so moving, light and funny but everyone could see how upset Jase was about the death. And Doug's had been really moving too.

Harley was definitely going to have to keep an eye on his best friend later on because he had no idea that Doug was this upset before now. He would have liked to have Doug sitting on the opposite side of him but he was also holding his mother's hand.

The silence of the field was great and everyone was hanging onto every single word of Thomas as he spoke on behalf of Harley's family. He didn't know half of the things had happened between their two families but clearly Grandma Craycraft had bought his parents a lot of joy over the years.

"And that is why I no longer take my umbrella outside because Craycraft would always steal it," his dad said.

Everyone laughed and Harley was really looking forward to returning home when he could see his parents every day. He could catch up with them and actually be a part of their lives.

As much as Harley loved university, Doug and the social life he had, he still sort of felt divorced from his own family and the rest of the world. There was such a bubble at university, especially if it was a campus university, so he sort of felt separated from what was happening in his family as the funeral proved.

And he just didn't want that anymore. He wanted to laugh, go out and just be with his family.

It was going to be even more amazing now they were going to get a dog. Harley was surprised that his mum had managed to wear down his dad about it because his mum had been banging on about it for years, and his dad had always firmly said no.

At least they were finally going to get a brand-new member of the family that he could walk, play with and love every day now that he was going to be home in Canterbury.

Harley bit his lip as he also realised that what he wanted also took him further away from Jase, the wonderful person he wanted more than anything else in the world. He wanted to love, treasure and be with the man he loved (it was only now he was realising just how he felt) but that meant dropping his Masters and not moving back to Canterbury with family and he wasn't going to do that.

Not for everyone and no matter how much he loved them.

Harley just closed his eyes slightly and focused on the great feeling of Jase's slightly rough, warm hands against his. He wanted to remember how great, right and natural this felt in case this was one of the last times he ever had to do it.

"You okay babe?" Jase asked.

Harley opened his eyes and felt a cold hard lump form in his throat. He just didn't want this to end, and they still had another day yet but it was only that.

A single day of joy, pleasure and love.

And then they would leave each other and perhaps never see one another ever again.

"Tonight can we plan how this is going to work after this weekend?" Harley asked, straining each word as he realised that they were in a serious relationship that might end in heartbreak.

The very worse kind of pain.

"Of course," Jase said. "I want this to work as much as you do and I want to move heaven and earth for you because I really, really like you. But let's enjoy today and talk about this later,"

Harley slowly nodded. He wasn't sure if he was getting what he wanted or if Jase was brushing him off and this was exactly why he never wanted to enter a relationship at a funeral anyway.

Relationships were next to impossible at the best of times but at a funeral, emotions were running high, focuses were on different things and more. What if Jase was only in a relationship with him because he wanted a distraction from his grandma's death?

Harley felt his mother move next to him. "I can tell he likes you, just relax dear and everything will be fine," his mum said.

Harley weakly smiled and squeezed both their hands tighter and he just hoped beyond hope that they were right.

Because Harley really had no idea how he could enjoy his Masters and the rest of his life knowing that the man he loved was on the opposite side of the country and there was nothing he could do about it.

GAY ROMANCE COLLECTION VOLUME 4

CHAPTER 12
Saturday 8th July 2023
Canterbury, England

Jase had had the best afternoon and early evening in his entire life, they entire family and all of Grandma Craycraft's friends had ditched the original plan and had decided to have a massive crazy party in the field, that now it was happening he was fairly sure all the hundreds of her friends had always planned it like that.

Jase leant against the large, rough, warm bark of an oak tree at the edge of the field and just wanted a few moments to himself away from all the speakers, people and everything that he had been enjoying for the last few hours.

He had to admit that all her friends had done a truly amazing job at transforming the field at such "short notice", the massive green field had two huge white marquees filled with plastic tables so people could sit and eat and rest their weary feet after a good dance.

The area outside the marquees were covered in four large black speakers had pounded out all sorts of great music from the 60s towards to the even better hits of today, something that Grandma Craycraft was surprisingly into.

And everyone was having a great time.

Jase had never seen so many people laughing, singing and dancing before. Anything he had seen at university was totally outdone by this party and it was amazing, really beautifully amazing.

A perfect tribute to an extraordinary woman.

"Your boyfriend's had a nice day," Douglas said as he came down the hill towards Jase and they both leant against the tree.

"I'll go and see him a moment, I just wanted a few moments to myself. Everyone's done her proud I think," Jase said.

"Of course, she would have loved this and she would have been a nightmare to bring home tonight,"

Jase just laughed. She really would have been and he would have felt sorry for the poor soul who had to force Grandma into a taxi to take her back.

"How are you doing?" Jase asked wanting to make sure his cousin was okay.

Douglas asked. "I just had this talk with Harley. He is amazing but I'm honestly doing okay now I've spoken to Harley. He does love you and I mean *love* you,"

Jase bit his lower lip. That was always exactly

what he didn't want to hear, he of course felt extremely strongly about Harley and there wasn't a single man he would rather spend the rest of his life with but calling it *love* was so dangerous considering they were going home tomorrow.

"I do really like him but how, how can we make this work?" Jase asked. "I want me and him to last so damn much but I don't know. I just don't want to hurt him,"

Douglas nodded and he looked like was going to have a sip of a drink he didn't have yet. "And that is the meaning of love or at least the potential. Just talk to him, tell him how you feel and more,"

"I just don't want to have to leave,"

Douglas leant closer to Jase. "That won't be easy because we're not going back tomorrow. Our leases at the uni aren't up until August so we're staying for another week here at Harley's parents and then we're going back,"

Jase just shook his head. "I wish I could stay for another week but I have work,"

Douglas took a few steps away and Jase really wanted to keep talking to him. He really liked talking to his family and he was desperate for some inspiration to his romance problem.

"What would Grandma do?" Douglas asked as he walked away.

Jase just laughed because that wasn't the sort of answer he wanted. Grandma Craycraft was a hell of a woman who knew exactly how to get what she wanted in life including romance, Jase wasn't that sort of person.

He knew that Grandma had met grandad on a cruise in the 60s when they were both still basically teens or what some people called "new adults" but he didn't know much more than that. Grandad had always told the story as she wore him down until he agreed to a date out of weakness.

The very last thing he wanted to do was basically bully Jase into staying with him or pulling him back to Bath, somewhere he didn't want to go.

Jase just huffed. This was going to be a nightmare conversation to have and he really was going to put it off until the last moment of tonight.

For now though he was going to go back, dance with the man he really liked and he was going to give Harley the best night he had ever had.

And hopefully that would lead to a little more adult celebration tonight. Anything to put off a conversation that Jase knew would be the hardest one of his life.

And that included his coming out conversation with his parents.

CHAPTER 13
Saturday 8th July 2023
Canterbury, England

Harley laughed and kissed Jase as they both stumbled into their hotel room later in the night, they weren't drunk but Harley had seriously loved just how amazing tonight had been.

As they both fell onto their larger double bed and Harley rested in his head on Jase's perfectly defined and sexy chest, he couldn't believe how lucky he was.

Harley really couldn't remember a better day of his life, he had laughed so much, danced and made out with the man he loved and it had just been such a sensational day that he never wanted to end.

He rolled over and faced the beautiful man he loved and Harley kissed him hard. Still loving the great taste of his soft full lips.

Harley was about to grab a manly feature but Jase stopped him and just looked at him. Harley had had a feeling this serious talk was going to happen tonight but he had just been so focused on enjoying tonight that he had hoped Jase had forgotten about it.

But the talk had to happen at some point no matter how much he didn't want it to.

Jase moved over slightly in the bed and Harley laid down next to him still resting his head on Jase's perfect chest.

"I don't want us to break up tomorrow," Jase said.

And Harley honestly expected to feel more relieved but he actually felt more anxious. His heart was beating faster, his throat was turning dry and his brain was travelling even fast as it struggled to find a solution.

But there wasn't one. At not one he could see.

"We can both get each other's number, we call each other three times a week, we'll text every day and night and we'll see each other once a month or something," Jase said. "We will be fine,"

Harley just nodded because he honestly had no idea what would come out. He didn't want to say something he would regret but he also didn't want something to upset him.

This wasn't ideal and it sounded like a good plan, it was some kind of progress after all.

Jase took out his phone and took a random photo and Harley just laughed because he looked like some kind of puppy on Jase's chest. Then Jase saved it as his lock screen and home screen.

"See I'll never forget you," Jase said.

Harley said the same and he really loved their picture. He would never be able to forget the man he loved now and there would always be a reminder whenever he went on his phone that he needed to text or call the man he loved.

But he had also heard a ton of stories of long-distance relationships from his friends, family and even today at the funeral some of the old gals were talking about their past relationships.

They always failed.

Harley kissed Jase savouring that perfectly seductive taste as he realised that Jase was like a Greek god, he was slightly older than him and Bath was a very popular city filled with tons of wonderful boys.

Jase would easily find someone again and what if that was for the best? What if it was cruel putting Jase through that much pain and emotion of missing him when he could be enjoying another man?

Jase sat up slightly and hugged Harley. "I will never leave you. I really, really like you,"

Harley weakly smiled and maybe that was just a sign of how great they were together. They had known each other for about a day and they could already read each other's thoughts.

His parents had always said that when you meet the right person you always know and it's basically love at first sight. That was exactly how he felt about Jase but it wasn't clear if Jase was the same way.

Harley pulled up the calendar app on his phone.

"Here, do you know when you start your DClinPsych? And when you're free?"

Jase frowned slightly. "I know when it starts but you know how it is. You don't know your routine or timetable until you get there,"

Harley wasn't keen on that but he knew that Jase wasn't lying to him. It was annoying as hell about university and yet it was what happened and they couldn't even plan when they were first going to meet up in September/ October.

Jase pulled Harley up so sharply he gasped.

"I know this is scary and everything seems doomed but we will find away," Jase said.

As Jase started kissing his neck, Harley couldn't help but realise that he didn't say *love finds a way* or give him anything more concrete.

"Was this just a distraction for you from your grandma's death?" Harley asked.

Jase shook his head and kept kissing Harley and then Jase moved his hands slower and slower and Harley moaned in pleasure.

But the fact that Jase never replied with words bothered him a hell of a lot more than he ever thought possible and now he was really questioning if Jase was better off without him.

CHAPTER 14
Sunday 9th July 2023
Canterbury, England

The next morning Jase, sexy Harley and Douglas met in a local café in the heart of Canterbury. It was always so magical on a Sunday morning because there was never a single student in sight because they were all recovering from the night before.

They all sat around a small black metal table and the delightful aromas of crispy bacon, waffles and maple syrup filled the air. There weren't many people in the café and Jase wrapped his hands around the large coffee mug he had.

He subtly watched as Harley ate his huge pancakes covered in chocolate sauce, maple syrup and some whipped cream. He was so cute and last night both of them had really given the other their all and Jase couldn't deny just how much he liked Harley.

He really was the one for him.

But Jase still couldn't get Harley's words about

him using Harley as a distraction out of his head. They were so wrong, flat out wrong but he couldn't believe that Harley had actually thought about them in the first place.

He knew both of them were scared about today but he hadn't clearly just how scared Harley actually was. They hadn't really spoken about past boyfriends except for Michael so he doubted Harley had had too many bad breaks, but what if Jase did have relationship problems?

Jase forced down a gasp as he realised that Michael might have actually been right. What if he wasn't ready for a serious relationship and Harley was?

Jase shook his head and he felt so guilty and confused and he really just didn't know what he wanted any more.

Before this weekend, he had been so dead set on doing his DClinPsych in Bath so he could become a clinical psychologist and help people, but he also really wanted Harley. He couldn't have both.

"You okay there?" Douglas asked.

Jase didn't even look at Douglas, he just looked at the man he really liked.

"I want to cancel everything but I can't," Jase said just letting the words flow out of his mouth. "You were never a distraction to me, you were the best thing that has ever happened to me. I hate that today is happening,"

Harley grinned but then he went back to stabbing

his pancakes and Jase doubted Harley was going to be looking up at him again.

"You are amazing, hot and great but I can't get in the way of your dreams," Harley said. "We both do clinical, we both know how much the country needs Clinical psychologists so you have to go to Bath and I'll join you in a year,"

Jase smiled but both him and Harley that was a very white lie. It was a famous fact that DClinPsych were extremely hard to get onto and the chance of Harley getting onto one without any work experience was next to nothing.

Sure he could still come down to Bath but there was more chance of him getting on a DClinPsych down here in Canterbury because it was always easier for students that were already at the university to get on the courses. Sometimes even without experience.

"You will make it work," Douglas said hugging Harley. "I will make sure it does, I got you two together and I'll keep you together,

"Why do you even care about us?" Jase asked out of frustration at their life, world and their doomed relationship.

Harley sat up perfectly straight but Jase could see that he understood the question and wasn't mad at him asking it.

"Because you're both the best people I know. You've helped me being gay more than I can ever repay you, I just want to do something nice for you both. You both deserve to be together,"

Jase leant against the table and took Harley's hand but Harley didn't take it and he stood up instead.

Harley stood in front of Jase. "You are the best, hottest man I know and you can do so much better than me. You can meet another hot guy that deserves you and isn't a rake like me. Enjoy Bath, become a psychologist and help people,"

Jase was just stunned as Harley kissed him on the lips and Jase made sure to infuse the memory of the feel, tongue and passion in the kiss for a final time because this would be it.

And as Harley ran out of the café crying Jase knew he thought that this was a mercy but it seriously felt like anything but. Jase felt like he had just been shot in the heart.

CHAPTER 15
Monday 10th July 2023
Canterbury, England

The next morning Harley sat on the large black kitchen island that his parents had recently installed in their very new kitchen with a bright rose gold fridge, oven and cabinets. He wrapped his hands around a very cold mug of coffee and he just stared into the pitch darkness that he felt was similar to his own life.

All he wanted was the black abyss of something to claim him.

The rest of the day yesterday had been awful and he was such an idiot. He had been wanting to give Jase a mercy and he just wanted what was best for the man he loved and sometimes that really was just letting him go so he could live a better life.

A better life without him.

"You were stupid yesterday," Doug said walking into the kitchen in just his black boxers, and even now as nice as Doug's body was it just wasn't as great as Jase's.

Last night had been good with Doug and him watching a film and Harley's parents had said both of them could stay as long as they wanted. They were both sad that Jase wouldn't be a member of the family but they understood his reasons.

Both Harley and Doug had slept together in his old bed like how they used to after late nights out at university, and he really didn't sit right with Harley that Doug should sleep on the floor considering he was trying (and failing) to make him feel better.

Clearly Doug had decided to change tactic.

Doug made himself a sweet spicy scented chai latte from their coffee machine and stood opposite Harley.

"I know that pose and you want to argue with me," Harley said.

"Of course I do. You were an idiot yesterday, hell both of you were. You were stupid for just giving this a try and you gave into your fear and he was an idiot for not running after you,"

"Well us two could always give it a go," Harley said, mockingly.

Doug shook his head. "You know I always would but we are best friends nothing more and you are in love with my cousin. That is what's happening,"

Harley took a sip of the bitter coffee. "And that's another reason, he's your cousin. That's surely wrong,"

Doug threw his hands up in the air. "Tell me

right now what's actually going on or we're no longer friends,"

Harley just looked at him. He hated the very notion of that idea but this was exactly how good of a friend Doug was, he was willing to sacrifice their friendship if it meant Harley would be happy in the future.

"I… I just don't want him to get hurt," Harley said. "Long distance relationships are hard, impossible even so what right do I have to enter one with him and hurt a great guy when he could be happy with someone else?"

Doug laughed. "You didn't want to hurt the guy but you broke up with him in a public place after he had confessed a lot to you,"

Harley bit his lower lip. "Well when you put it like that I do sound like an idiot,"

Doug took a large sip of his chai latte and shook his head probably because the drink was too hot.

"Now what are you going to do about it?" Doug asked.

Harley finished his own coffee and paced around the kitchen for a moment. He needed to see Jase immediately and he needed to apologise and say that he too was going to move heaven and earth.

And then he realised something.

"I've just realised that I was focusing too much on words. He might not have been saying very emotional things to me, but he was *doing* tons of things to me,"

"I bet he was,"

Harley playfully Doug over the head. "Please drive me to Bath,"

Doug folded his arms and looked around like he actually had better things to do and he was rearranging his day entirely.

"Please," Harley said actually getting on both knees and basically begging him. It was only then that he realised just how badly he wanted, needed this.

"Fine," Doug said grinning. "Let me take a shower and we'll be on the road in half an hour,"

"Thank you," Harley said hugging and kissing Doug on the cheek.

Harley went upstairs to pack a small bag because he actually had no idea how long he would be staying in Bath but there was no hope in hell he was leaving without having Jase as his boyfriend.

CHAPTER 16
Monday 10th July 2023
Canterbury, England

As much as Jase loved having Fanny come home with him after the funeral and the six hours yesterday driving back had been great fun filled with laughter, great stories and excitement, he couldn't get beautiful sexy Harley out of his head.

Jase stood at the large kitchen window in his little flat in the heart of Bath that cost him an arm and both legs per month (another benefit of having Fanny move in with him for now), and just stared out at the views of the city he really loved.

Bath had some amazing architecture, cobblestone streets and the sky was bright and clear. Normally Jase would have loved a day like this one but he didn't, he really didn't at all because the man he really liked was thousands of miles away.

"You should have at least chased after him," Fanny said.

Jase turned around and went to join Fanny at their small wooden dinner table/ desk/ coffee table (it was a small flat after all) and he even helped himself to a piece of crispy bacon that Fanny had cooked for herself. She had offered to do him some too but Jase flat out wasn't in the mood to eat at the moment.

All he could do was think about Harley's fit body, perfect smile and just, he was a wonderful man.

"I probably should have but it's over. Harley made that very clear," Jase said.

"Prove him wrong. Chase him down. Confess your love for him,"

Jase just looked at her. "I can't do that and I have work later. I couldn't do any of that even if I wanted to. And you cannot *love* someone after only a weekend,"

Fanny leant back. "Of course you can. I love you from the moment I popped out of mum's stomach. I loved you after a second, why can't you love Harley after a few million seconds?"

Jase just had no idea what to say to that. He really did love his sister but it was amazing that she was a high-profile investment banker. Maybe she changed her brain when she was working?

"Jase, please just do something about your relationship. Because you are driving me insane, do you remember what you did last time?"

Jase shrugged.

"Exactly, you did nothing but just sit in front of

the TV and hog it. I wanted to watch reality rubbish and all you wanted to watch was documentaries that you weren't even paying attention to. Do you know how infuriating that is?"

Jase smiled as he had sort of done that on purpose to annoy her like every big brother should but he did get the point.

Jase took out his phone and realised that his hands were shaking.

"What would I even say?" Jase asked.

Fanny took a massive bit out of her bacon like she was mulling over the answer and needed to buy herself a few more seconds, probably just another banker tactic, but it seemed to work.

"I don't know, maybe you should go classical like *I love you and you're the best thing that's ever happened to me,*"

Jase went to his contacts and dialled Harley's number. It went straight to voicemail so Harley had either blocked him, denied his call or simply didn't want to talk to him.

Jase stumbled onto the seat opposite Fanny and she just rolled her eyes and took out her own phone.

"Here," Fanny said passing him her phone.

Jase had no idea what it was because when they were growing up Fanny was super protective of her phone, he doubted the habit had changed, so this was a right honour.

He read the phone screen and it was something about postgraduate students at Jase's university being able to recommend future students for the following academic year. It was a trial programme because the university felt that academic-only references in the application process was a little snobby.

"I've contacted a friend of mine in the accounting department, preliminary results show recommended students are really likely to get selected," Fanny said as she stood up.

Jase just grinned because this basically meant that him and Harley would only be away from each other for one academic year, and they could see each other in the month-long Easter and Christmas breaks.

They could be together and their relationship would work, be strong and definitely survive this.

"I also called your boss, another friend of mine and I'm covering your shift tonight. It's amazing the people you meet in a banking job. Bye," Fanny said.

Jase just couldn't believe how amazing his sister was, he actually believed her to be a horrible Pitbull that would interrogate all his boyfriends but maybe the years of travelling abroad had mellowed her out a little.

And now she really wanted Jase to have everything she didn't have at the moment.

Jase grabbed his coat and keys and he was going to get back to Canterbury and talk to the man he *loved*.

CHAPTER 17
Monday 10th July 2023
Canterbury, England

Jase hopped into his small black Fiat and didn't even allow the burning hot black seats to bother him as he just had to get to Canterbury to see the man he really loved. And he couldn't believe he was actually thinking the words, it wasn't logical, wise or rational to fall in love with Harley but he had.

And he didn't want that to change for anything.

Jase started driving and a few minutes later he was out driving along the wide chaotic motorways of southern England with the largely empty grey road ahead of him. The road that would lead him to his heart and his love.

Massive fields of green grass lined the motorway with the odd sheep and cow dotting them. And he felt so happy to be alive, in love and free to do what he wanted in life.

Michael was definitely wrong about them because

it was only Michael that wasn't capable of being in a long-term relationship. But there was nothing more that Jase wanted, needed in the entire world. He didn't care about his career, grades or anything as long as he had the man he loved next to him.

A few hours later, the large cathedral spire of Canterbury appeared in the distance like a weird beacon of hope and way marker that Jase drove towards and it wasn't too long until he hit the Canterbury traffic.

Jase had no idea what the problem was up ahead but Jase didn't care. His love was in the city and he didn't mind sitting in his car on a little narrow road that wasn't moving. The small white houses with their fresh clean paint looked almost as great as Jase felt.

As the traffic slowly started moving Jase couldn't believe that he noticed a familiar car up ahead, he could have sworn it was Douglas's little black Ford that was still sitting there. It made no sense why he was in the lane of traffic leaving the city.

Harley had always said that him and Douglas were leaving next week so why were they trying to leave Canterbury?

The traffic started moving but Jase didn't care.

He stopped the car and almost had another car ram into the back of him and he ran out of his car towards the black Ford.

Before he could reach the Ford that was now moving, the passenger side door popped open and Harley jumped out of the slowly moving car.

Everyone was honking their horns and Jase and Harley just laughed as they saw each other. They both ran at each other and hugged and kissed.

Jase just loved the wonderful feeling of Harley's fit, sexy body in his arms and he never ever wanted to let the man he loved go ever again.

"I love you Harley. I love you," Jase said.

Harley's eyes turned wet and they both started laughing again.

"Guys," Douglas said. "You want to drive away before this traffic gets much worse. We've been trying to leave Canterbury for hours,"

Jase laughed again and grabbed Harley's smooth hand and they both ran towards Jase's car and they drove off together but he was a little surprised that everyone had loved honking their horns.

Maybe that was a sign that everyone else also knew as soon as they saw the two of them together that they were meant to be, and as chaotic as the world was at times everyone knew deep down that when you saw two people in love, you were meant to help them at all costs.

And as Jase drove deeper into Canterbury, he just couldn't believe how lucky he was. He was with the man he loved, he was cut out for long-term relationships unlike Michael and in September he would be starting his doctorate.

Life really didn't get much better than that and Jase honestly wasn't sure that he wanted it too. Especially as him and Harley held hands the entire way to the car park. And Jase couldn't believe how great, right and natural it felt.

Jase really was living his best life and that was a wonderful feeling to have.

CHAPTER 18
Canterbury, England

Five years later, Harley sat on the edge of a beautifully wide open lake in the middle of the Lake District with the soft thick grass under him, the sound of crickets and the people partying in the distance echoed around the lakes and the man he loved close against him.

Harley loved it how Jase, his husband, rested his head on his shoulders and Harley still couldn't believe how great the last five years had been. They were both now doctors of clinical psychology and both had jobs they loved working with people with various mental health conditions. They were improving lives and helping people and Harley had to admit nothing really came close to that feeling.

And after five years together, Harley had been so, so happy when Jase had asked him to be his husband. Of course Harley said yes immediately and even he was surprised he didn't hesitate but that was just how perfect the past five years had been.

Every single moment they were together was filled with so much joy, love and passion that Harley was amazed that it hadn't died out yet but this was what love really felt like. Harley hated being away from his love but that only made their time together even more special.

Just like tonight.

The lake ahead of them was shrouded in darkness with the bright moonlight gently shining, a nice cool refreshing breeze blew past them and caused minor ripples on the glassy surface. All their friends, family and their plus-ones were in a marquee (that the local council had been very keen on for some reason) and were having a blast.

Harley was actually just enjoying this moment of peace on his wedding day. Doug was his best man and he had done the best speech he had ever heard, he had done a great job organising the wedding and Doug really had been their rock. Weddings were stressful things after all.

It was even better that Doug was getting married next month to a wonderful man, Evan, he had met doing his own Masters course. And Harley couldn't be happier for his best friend, Evan definitely was a lucky guy.

"Did you ever think we would be doing this?" Jase asked.

Harley laughed. "No but I'm glad we did. I've glad we were both willing to drive to the other side of the country and almost miss each other to prove our love,"

Harley just pulled Jase's soft muscular body against him even more. He flat out knew he was never going to be tired of feeling and exploring that perfect body of Jase's.

"And just think, this never would have happened without Grandma Craycraft," Jase said.

Harley smiled at that. It was very well and even after the funeral, Harley was still surprised at all the stories he had found out about that wonderfully strange and joyous woman. She helped to play matchmaker, she donated so much money to charity and even had thankfully fostered ten children over the course of her life.

She was all about making sure people had the best lives they possibly could, and Harley seriously respected her because she was amazing.

"But I'm not sure I'm taking the name Craycraft," Harley said. "It's too long,"

Jase laughed and pulled Harley down so they were both laying on the ground together.

Harley kissed his husband. "I'm serious. Cole is so much easier to say and write down,"

Jase shook his head. "We'll talk about this tomorrow, Doctor Cole, but, honestly babe I would be nothing without you,"

Harley kissed Jase the hardest he had all day. "Me too,"

"Love birds you coming back!" Doug shouted.

Harley laughed and buried his head on Jase's well-defined chest and shook his head. "Maybe if we remain still for long enough they'll go away,"

Jase kissed on the head and started to pull himself up. "Not a chance and I would like another dance with you Doctor,"

Harley just shrugged pretending like that was the worst thing imaginable "Well when you put it like that Doctor Craycraft I would love to,"

As the two of them went back to their wedding reception, Harley's stomach filled with butterflies because this wasn't the ending of a great five-year journey filled with love, romance and passion. This was the start of an even better journey of marriage and Harley was really excited to see where that would lead them.

It would only lead to great new things but Harley couldn't deny how much he had loved Jase from the moment they first met and he knew without a shadow of a doubt their love would never die.

And there wasn't a single better feeling than the feeling of true love. The exact same emotion both him and his husband were experiencing now and forever for the rest of their wonderful lives.

LOVE BETRAYS YOU

CONNOR WHITELEY

No part of this book may be reproduced in any form or by any electronic or mechanical means. Including information storage, and retrieval systems, without written permission from the author except for the use of brief quotations in a book review.

This book is NOT legal, professional, medical, financial or any type of official advice.

Any questions about the book, rights licensing, or to contact the author, please email connorwhiteley@connorwhiteley.net

Copyright © 2024 CONNOR WHITELEY

All rights reserved.

CHAPTER 1
6ᵗʰ May 2023
Rochester, England

MI5 Intelligence Officer Marcus Dawson had sat on his favourite grey camping chair with just the right levels of support in all the right places as he sat to one side of the huge football in front of him. The large thick white lines of the pitch had been freshly painted and even though he knew next to nothing about football he still loved helping out.

Marcus smiled as he watched his big brother, Ryan, run about in his bright blue football jersey with tons of little eight-year-olds kids running after him and after the football at the same time.

He had to admit that the weather was perfect for a Saturday morning kick about and coaching session. Marcus wasn't really sure why his brother had wanted the help because Ryan had always been brilliant with kids, but if it meant he got to see more of his brother between "business trips" then he certainly wasn't going to complain at all.

The day was crisp and warm and the bright sunshine bathed the football in a perfect golden light that really made Marcus smile. It was a perfect summer day and he hadn't received a single call from MI5 for a few days, so hopefully everything was right with the world.

Or as right as they could be when you had Russia, China and the middle east all looking for any weakness in the UK to exploit. Some days Marcus couldn't decide if the UK's enemies were just being stupid or they were just useless at their jobs.

It wasn't exactly hard to find a weakness in the UK.

Marcus smiled as the smell aromas of sausage rolls, pizza and tacos filled the air from the nearby food truck that always set up shop behind him in the car park. He was so looking forward to having lunch with his brother and they could catch up about Ryan, his wife and their three beautiful children.

Marcus would have loved to have a kid or boyfriend of his own but that was the problem with intelligence work, it was flat out impossible to meet people. And it was even harder to stay together. It was normally the secrets, the lies and the tension from the missions that always killed a relationship in the end.

"Watch out," someone said.

Marcus moved his head slightly as a football flew past him.

Marcus laughed, got the ball and kicked it back onto the football pitch. It was so worth helping out just so he could see the grins and shouts of happiness from the little kids.

They really did love it here.

"So this is what you do when you don't want to come to work," a woman said behind him.

Marcus smiled as he turned around and saw his best friend in the entire world and handler, Madame Aria Roaings. Marcus couldn't deny she looked great in her long black trench coat, black hat and black high heels. She had to be baking inside given the heat of the late morning but Marcus was never going to argue with her.

"It's nice you still keep in touch with your brother," Aria said.

Marcus wanted to hug her but he didn't dare. Aria was way too emotionless and cold for that to happen. He still didn't like being reminded of how Aria's kids and entire family and husband believed she had died years ago in a plane crash.

It was simply safer that way for everyone and it meant she could move a lot more freely in the shadows of the world.

"I love my brother and I take it you're not going to let me enjoy lunch with him," Marcus said knowing the answer already.

Aria allowed a rare smile to crack her lips. "Of course I'll allow you but I thought you might want the extra time to prepare for an important task. And I hope you own a tux,"

Marcus grinned. He always loved missions that required him to dress up, it wasn't so much so that he liked looking amazing himself. It was more the fact that if he needed to dress up nicely then so did a lot of other insanely hot men.

Men in suits looked sensational. Marcus was always hard at the thought of it.

"What's the job?" Marcus asked waving at Ryan as he ran past with the kids just chasing him now.

"Two days ago the UK's latest advancement in communication jamming software was stolen. It's called Blackout for a reason and-"

Marcus nodded. "I've heard of the software before. Can it really Blackout all of the US if placed and activated in the right location?"

"Exactly," Aira said. "Every single TV screen, telephone, mobile phone and more across the entire USA could be knocked out for days if Blackout was activated. And that means a hell of a lot of European countries could be knocked out too,"

"I think it's safe to presume that is not the reason we're going after Blackout," Marcus said smiling because he knew full well the UK Government couldn't have cared less about mainland Europe.

"True," Aria said smiling as a kid ran past, stopped to look at her and then ran off again.

"Where am I going then?"

"There's a party tonight in Canterbury being hosted by one of the top families in the UK and it's an auction for Blackout. All the various Intelligence services and terrorism organisations throughout the world will be there to get their hands on it,"

"You need me to go in there, get Blackout and kill whoever took it in the first place," Marcus said.

"Negative. Get Blackout get out. We cannot kill anyone at that party because it is too high profile. Blackout is my only concern and I'll send you the details of what it looks like in a moment. Can you handle it?"

Marcus laughed. He could always handle a simple retrieval mission. Marcus couldn't believe it would be that hard to go into a mansion or wherever the party was being held, get Blackout out without anyone realising and simply slip back into the night.

It wasn't hard.

But Marcus was looking forward to seeing all those hot sexy men in their tight black suits a lot more than he ever wanted to admit.

Tonight was going to be a lot of fun.

CHAPTER 2
6th May 2023
Canterbury, England

Aden Grant didn't exactly consider himself a bad person, a bad man or something who enjoyed anything about his father's family business. He saw himself as more of a "getting the job done" sort of man and given how his father had fostered him, adopted him and given him everything when his own parents had abandoned him as a child.

Aden really didn't see the harm in simply getting a few slightly illegal items for his father.

He took a wonderfully cool crystal glass of champagne as the hot male waiter in his very tight black suit came round the immense circular hall the guests had been stuffed into. It was hardly the best, but not the worst, party he had ever been to.

Aden rather liked the seriously tall white textured walls that reminded him of chapels and various religious buildings that might have been crappy, but even hateful religion can be beautiful at times.

High above the guests was a beautiful chandelier that Aden had never really been fussed with before, but there was just something about how this one was shining like diamonds high in the ceiling, that he really liked. Then he realised the chandelier did have diamonds on it and if the hall was a little less empty he might have actually tried to steal them.

He never knew when his father might need some diamonds for the business.

Aden nodded his hellos to a very cute man in a slightly loose-fitting black suit with a blond beard, brown shoes and a beautiful smile. The entire hall might have been packed with hot straight men but Aden couldn't deny the fact everyone looked beautiful in their suits.

And even the slim, cold and more probably assassin women attached to their arms looked very attractive to. They all had their blue, red and black dresses and Aden wasn't sure if the women in their dresses were trying to stand out or not.

He was definitely going to have to focus on them because it was only the sexist "official" government agencies that believed women were weak and stupid. Aden seriously knew from personal experience that women were a lot more dangerous than men when it came to these sorts of events.

And Aden had already recognised at least twenty internationally wanted criminals here and another forty intelligence officers from all over the world. It seemed that everyone wanted Blackout but Aden wasn't going to let that happen.

Only he was walking away from Blackout.

"And who are you?"

Aden looked around to see a rather pretty young woman in a black dress standing there, he knew her. Why his father had sent Isabella along too was a pain in the neck. He loved her as a foster sister but this wasn't right. This was his mission, his right and his chance to prove himself.

"Relax little bro," Isabella said taking his champagne glass and downing it in one. "Father trusts you. He really does but Blackout is too important to let slip so we are working together,"

"You make that sound like a bad thing,"

Isabella smiled. "The one that shot me in the ass last year,"

Aden laughed. He still had no idea how he had managed that but now she had mentioned it, Aden focused on the way that everyone was walking.

It was a little-known fact that even the most powerful, experienced and lethal intelligence officers always moved slightly differently depending on whether they were packing a gun or not, or even knives.

Aden always preferred knives to guns because they were a lot more fun and exciting and interesting, but it seemed everyone else here was a lot more interested in guns.

"I do have a spare Glock if you want it," Isabella

said.

"You know I don't do guns,"

Isabella laughed. "And one day that will be the death of you little brother. Now I will leave you because we need to keep our association unknown and if someone else wins flirt and get with them,"

"Of course but what if it's a woman?"

"Really?" Isabella asked laughing. "You're gay and most of these people are straight. You were always doing to have to get with a woman tonight,"

"What about you getting with a man?"

Isabella grinned that maddening smile that made Aden's stomach churn and curdle. "Apparently I'm too scary for hookups,"

Aden smiled because he didn't doubt that for a second considering she always killed her boyfriends in short order.

He watched her walk away and he noticed there was a new person coming into the hall and-

Wow. Fuck. Fuck. Fuck.

Aden seriously wished he had a glass of champagne to down it the moment as he watched the most sensational, explosive, divine man he had ever met in his entire life stalk into the hall.

He had never seen a man with such confidence, such power and authority just walk into a hall and seem to dominate it. And the man in his extremely hot, sexy black suit that showed off his fit ass and his sexy insanely seductive body, Aden just didn't know what to do.

He was glued in place.

Aden wanted to run, hide or even go over and talk to the hottie but his body wasn't listening.

The man's face was insanely hot as Aden just focused on him. His strong jawline, short brown hair and his lifeful and hopeful eyes were so stunning Aden never wanted to look away.

Now Aden just hoped beyond hope that the mere presence of this hottie wasn't going to distract him because he had to get Blackout for his father no matter the cost.

So the best way to make sure the hottie didn't get Blackout was to make sure Aden was with him when the auction started.

And the hottie was alone so he might even be gay.

Aden just grinned at that amazing idea because that seriously would be sensational.

CHAPTER 3
6th May 2023
Canterbury, England

As Marcus went into the immense hall where the party and auction was happening he was certainly glad the hot, sexy men of the world's various intelligence services and criminal underworld had maintained their part of the bargain about looking hot in their nice tight black suits.

Intelligence officers and criminals seriously knew how to dress up great when they wanted to.

Marcus smiled at a young waitress as she passed him a glass of champagne, he had no intention of drinking it but it was all part of the show. It was good seeing so many old intelligence friends, both male and female, and old enemies in their suits and dresses.

The bright chandelier above looked wonderful and it made Marcus smile as he remembered fun missions in Italy, Spain and a whole bunch of other catholic countries with their stunning architecture. He

CHAPTER 3
6th May 2023
Canterbury, England

As Marcus went into the immense hall where the party and auction was happening he was certainly glad the hot, sexy men of the world's various intelligence services and criminal underworld had maintained their part of the bargain about looking hot in their nice tight black suits.

Intelligence officers and criminals seriously knew how to dress up great when they wanted to.

Marcus smiled at a young waitress as she passed him a glass of champagne, he had no intention of drinking it but it was all part of the show. It was good seeing so many old intelligence friends, both male and female, and old enemies in their suits and dresses.

The bright chandelier above looked wonderful and it made Marcus smile as he remembered fun missions in Italy, Spain and a whole bunch of other catholic countries with their stunning architecture. He didn't get to travel much because MI5 was only focused on the UK's internal security but every so often he got to travel abroad.

Something that he loved with all his heart.

The only feature of the hall he didn't like was the weird textured white walls, they just looked weird and out of place. Something was wrong with them but Marcus couldn't put his finger on it.

A group of women walked past Marcus and he just didn't understand them.

Marcus had no idea why the women wanted to wear bright red dresses because surely that would only draw attention to them. Or maybe that was the point, the eyes focused on the women in red dresses whilst the women in black dresses actually got the work done and stole Blackout.

He wasn't exactly sure how many of the people here tonight actually intended to steal Blackout or simply just pay for it like they were meant to. Marcus didn't want to pay for it because the UK Government would never have the money for it.

The country was broke as fuck after all, Marcus really couldn't understand why the UK should have to pay for their own equipment back?

It made no sense.

"There's half the criminal underworld in here," Jessica said in his earpiece.

Marcus was really glad that Jessica had given up her Saturday night to support him back at HQ and she was currently watching the room through a camera in one of his buttons.

"I know," Marcus said quietly, "just talk me through it all and I'll nod or something,"

"Look over there to your left. The man with the half-burnt head of hair. That is a Syrian militant leader wanted in fifty countries for terrorism, murder and genocide,"

Marcus nodded. He might want to take him out if given the chance.

"Then to your right if you look at the large elderly woman who is the director of the Chilean Security Service and she will kill everyone if she gets the chance,"

Marcus wasn't too bothered about her.

"And the man coming towards you is a nobody. There is no official record of him," Jessica said.

Marcus looked straight ahead and… oh. He seriously had a feeling that this mission was going to be fucked in short order.

Marcus could only stare with his mouth open at the utterly beautiful, stunning and outrageously hot man walking towards him so artfully, gracefully and silently that Marcus didn't doubt he was a perfect assassin.

It was fascinating and beautiful to watch the man glide through the crowd without touching, talking or disrupting a single person in the tightly packed room. And yet Marcus could see him and he was so beautiful.

Marcus wasn't sure exactly what made him so

stunning. It might have been his perfectly pointy jaw and his handsome face that made him all so young, baby-faced and cute. It could have been his fit as fuck body that didn't show any signs of muscles, body fat or anything.

But the guy was carrying a weapon.

He was walking too silently and gracefully for it to be a gun so Marcus was willing to bet knives. It was old-fashioned for sure but Marcus couldn't deny if a young man like himself was cool enough to enough knives instead of a gun then he was certainly a man worth talking too.

Marcus almost felt like a giant compared to the man as he walked a metre from him.

"You saw me," the man said in a deep, manly sexy voice. "Not a lot of people are able to see me through crowds."

"Not a lot of people carry knives these days. I prefer a Glock myself," Marcus said.

The man started walking circles around him and again the entire groups of people around him simply moved like they were being moved by a force they didn't know was affecting them.

"A Glock is too powerful, too quick, too loud," the man said. "Knives are quieter, more skilful and they get the job done. You have to be MI5?"

Marcus laughed. This man was good and really hot and beautiful.

"And before you ask it's the suit that gave you away. It is not an expensive Italian suit like a lot of what these men are wearing,"

"You aren't wearing silk either. Are you a government officer?"

Marcus didn't know why the beautiful man was laughing so much. It was a good question.

"Heavens no," the man said looking around so Marcus guessed he wasn't alone.

"Relax," Jessica said. "I'm looking through the camera footage now to see if anyone else is focusing on the man. Find out his name,"

"I'm Marcus. What about you?"

"Your government databases don't have me on there?" the man said offering Marcus his hand. "My name's Aden,"

Marcus took the man's hand and was seriously surprised by how warm, smooth and wonderful it was as he felt affection, chemistry and even a little sexual tension flow between them.

Then Aden flicked the suit button containing the camera and Marcus frowned as he knew the camera was broken.

"Shall we attend the auction?" Aden asked offering Marcus his arm.

Marcus had no idea at all who the hell this man was but he was beautiful, a little crazy and Marcus supposed as he was after Blackout too, Marcus really had to keep this hottie a lot closer than he normally would.

And that was hardly a problem at all.

CHAPTER 4
6th May 2023
Canterbury, England

Aden hadn't exactly intended to run into an MI5 officer whilst at the party but he was more than glad he had. Marcus had to be the hottest, most beautiful man he had ever seen and for someone from MI5 he was clearly intelligent. Something the officers he tended to come across seriously lacked.

Aden loved how smooth, warm and natural having Marcus on his arm felt. It had been a lot longer than Aden wanted to admit since he had time with a hot man and at least gotten the chance to show him off in public.

He led Marcus towards the very front of the hall were a small white stage had been erected and a podium was already up ready for the auction to begin. Everyone else in their blue, black and red dresses and sexy suits were tightly packed together because everyone was just waiting for the shit to hit the fan.

The entire problem with the hall was that there were only two exits. It wouldn't be hard for an enemy operative to secure them and then just kill them all and Aden really didn't like being limited by his options.

Aden subtly moved a hand down to his waist where he kept his knives because everything was very off here. There was a poor smell of sweat, fear and damp that clung to the air and made the awful taste of sweaty gym socks form on his tongue from where his real brothers used to bully him as a child.

Aden looked at beautiful Marcus and he just grinned at how cute he was. It was clear Marcus had worked out the same as him but it was probably because his tech support person couldn't see what they were seeing. He hadn't really meant to destroy the camera but he just had to protect his father, the family business and Isabella.

They had given him everything and he just wanted to protect them.

Then Aden noticed every single person in the room was subtly moving their hands towards their weapons.

"This is a setup," Aden said quietly to Marcus.

"By who and what would they want to gain?"

Aden smiled. "You have the world's top intelligence officers in these walls and the other half of the world's top criminals. Attack here and a hell of a lot of organisations become headless,"

"You still haven't told me who you work for?"

Aden was so tempted to reveal small parts of himself to this hot, beautiful man but that would be a deadly mistake. He couldn't afford to get attached, he couldn't afford love, he couldn't afford anything to do with Marcus.

But he would keep him alive for now.

"I don't see Blackout," Marcus said.

Aden waved him silent as an elderly woman went onto the stage wearing a sweeping blue dress and she stood at the podium.

"My dearest intelligence officers and wonderful criminals," the woman said. "I didn't want it to come to this but I have changed by mind about selling Blackout because it is simply too much fun to use,"

A whole bunch of criminals whipped out their guns. Aden had to admit the woman and the criminals were stupid unless the woman had a plan he hadn't figured out yet.

The woman unveiled her dress sleeves a little and revealed a large black watch containing all sorts of flashing lights, transmitters and God knows what. But that was Blackout or at least it was the control mechanism that the rest of Blackout ran off.

Whoever controlled that watch controlled the entire system.

Aden heard a lot of people at the back of the room shut the doors and seal them. Everyone else hadn't noticed it yet and he had to protect his family and Isabella and Marcus.

They had to get out now. This was a clusterfuck

and a half because everyone was about to get murdered.

"We have to go," Aden said.

Marcus whipped out his gun. "Not without Blackout. I have a mission,"

"Leave it. There's always another way. Don't die for nothing," Aden said taking out a knife.

He really didn't know a way out of here but through the crowds to their left about twenty metres away there was a second way out. The same way the woman had entered the stage from.

It was their only way.

"And just so no one can come after me as I set the world on fire you are all going to die," the woman said grinning.

Aden threw a knife at her.

It slammed into her chest.

Aden flicked his wrist and the tiny string on the knife made it fly back to him.

The entire hall went silent.

And the silence was replaced with the sound of a dragon roaring.

Missiles were incoming.

CHAPTER 5
6th May 2023
Canterbury, England

As much as Marcus flat out didn't know anything about beautiful Aden he really didn't want him to die.

The deafening roar of the incoming missiles roared overhead and Marcus grabbed the beautiful man next to him. They had to escape, get out of there and just forget about Blackout for now. Their lives were way too important.

Three missiles ripped into the building.

Marcus's ears rang.

Chunks of ceiling smashed down around them.

The chandelier shattered. Smashing down onto the floor.

People collapsed to the ground.

Marcus saw tons of people swarming towards the stage.

Machine guns fired.

Flames exploded everywhere.

A large group of men stormed out of the second entrance towards the murdered woman. They were going to retrieve Blackout.

Aden was about to throw a knife. Marcus grabbed his wrist.

"They're distracted. We leave now," Marcus said.

Aden rolled his eyes. A woman tackled Marcus to the ground.

He landed on a corpse.

The woman wrapped her hands round his throat. He recognised her. She was an old enemy.

A knife slammed into her head.

Marcus kicked the corpse off him.

More machine gun fire ripped through the audience.

Chunks of ceiling smashed down around them.

Flames poured from the ceiling.

Marcus charged.

Aden followed him.

Some of the machine gun men noticed.

Marcus fired his Glock.

Bullets screamed through the air.

Chests exploded.

Marcus went through the second entrance. He didn't know where he was going. He simply kept running down the silver corridor.

Marcus hooked a right.

Three women in black dresses jumped out. Firing pistols.

Marcus leapt to one side behind a kitchen door.

He fired blind. The women went to reload and Marcus looked out again ready to fire but Aden had already killed them all with his knives.

Marcus went over to Aden who was standing oddly close to the bodies pulling out his knives and Marcus had to admit he was impressed.

And now that he was finally standing behind Aden, Marcus definitely wasn't going to lie about how amazing Aden's ass looked in that nice tight suit.

Marcus aimed his Glock out ahead of them as him and Aden continued down the corridor and the icy cold draft and aroma of smoke and charred flesh told him that the exit was up ahead.

"What the hell happened here?" Marcus asked.

"I don't know. My father's organisation was simply requested to come here and was given the chance to bid on the item,"

Marcus shook his head. "They played us all for fools and idiots. I bet everyone in that damn room got a tip-off and it was a planned slaughter,"

Marcus checked an opening in the corridor for more enemies but it was empty and he noticed a large steel door ahead was open. Almost trying to lure them outside.

"We have to find out who the hell stole Blackout in the first place," Marcus said, "and then get it back,"

He heard Aden laugh behind him.

"What's so funny?" Marcus asked.

"That's MI5 job. My job's failed for now because I only wanted to come here tonight to get Blackout myself. I'm chasing nothing and come on this organisation clearly has money and resources,"

Marcus was about to comment when he heard footsteps run up behind him.

Marcus spun around. Silly Aden was frozen.

The woman fired.

Marcus tackled Aden.

Marcus ducked into a small storage room. Using the door as cover.

He fired. Again. Again.

The woman kept charging.

Marcus jumped out into the woman's rampage.

He saw her.

He fired.

She went down.

Thankfully he was okay and then he checked on beautiful Aden. He really hoped that he was okay and he wasn't injured. He knew he had only just met this beautiful man but Marcus really did want to see him more and more.

Aden smiled on the floor and then just stood up like nothing had ever happened.

"You know if you want to touch me you only have to ask. You don't need to tackle me to the ground,"

Marcus laughed and him and the beautiful man next to him simply went out of the steel door and out onto the cobblestone high street of Canterbury walking away from the ugly noise of police, counterterrorism and fire engine sirens.

After walking in silence for a few moments Marcus looked at Aden and pinned him up against the wall.

"Who are you?" Marcus asked.

He didn't trust him in the slightest and as much as Marcus just wanted to kiss and hug the stunning man something had happened tonight and Marcus had a feeling Aden knew a lot more than he was letting on.

"Why didn't you dive to one side when that woman attacked us?" Marcus asked. "You have the skills to notice something bad was about to happen in the hall but not when a woman is storming towards us,"

Aden grinned and kissed Marcus.

Marcus jumped in shock but he didn't stop the kiss. He didn't resist, he just enjoyed it and allowed the amazing mind-blowing feeling of Aden's full, tasty lips flow between them.

Aden seriously knew how to kiss.

Then Aden flipped himself over Marcus's shoulder so Marcus was now pinned against the wall.

"As much as I love intelligence games I have a family to get back to but I hope to see you again dearest Officer Marcus," Aden said giving him another kiss.

Marcus just turned around and watched Aden and his wonderful ass walk away off into the night. He had no idea who this man was but he was certainly beautiful, certainly clever and certainly up to something.

And that excited Marcus a lot more than he ever wanted to admit.

CHAPTER 6
6th May 2023
Canterbury, England

Aden was seriously not impressed that damn Isabella had tried to shoot at him and sexy Marcus. Of course the bullets weren't real, her death wasn't real and everything about the damn scene was fake as anything. But the attacked and murdered bodies they were very real and clearly whoever was behind all of this knew exactly what they were.

Aden went into the little apartment in the heart of Canterbury they were using as their safehouse for tonight only. It didn't exactly have a lot of stuff and Aden was wearing thick rubber gloves to avoid leaving any prints and tomorrow before they left they would clean the place so none of their DNA remained.

Aden looked at the black sofa, ugly wooden dining table with a wobbly leg and single still-standing dining chair and he just went to sit on it. The other dining chair had broken early because Isabella had sat on it whilst she was cleaning her Glock, Aden had laughed and she had only smiled.

It was those little moments that Aden loved about his family, because he was part of something and it was nice that his family respected him, loved him and wanted to support him no matter what.

The awful smell of rotten meat, rotten vegetables and cat wee filled the air as Isabella came out from the bathroom. And Aden was going to be so glad to get rid of this place tomorrow but they had still failed.

Aden wasn't sure what the plan was now. They could easily go out again and try to find out what was happening with Blackout and try again. Or Aden wasn't sure if Father already had another job for them so he needed them back sooner rather than later.

Isabella just grinned at him as she sat on the dining table.

"It's a shame he didn't shoot you," Aden said smiling.

Aden went over and hugged Isabella because it was good that she was okay but he would have rather she hadn't seen him with Marcus. The last thing he ever wanted her to believe was that Marcus was his weakness.

Aden wasn't sure if he was but he was so cute, innocent and handsome that Aden really wanted to spend more time with him.

"What now?" Aden asked. "I killed the woman but what happened to Blackout?"

Isabella grinned. "The machine gun idiots dealt with everyone else. You, me and your boy toy were the only survivors so the organisation the woman controlled has Blackout back,"

Aden hated it how she called Marcus his boy toy. He wouldn't have minded at all if that was the case but they had a job to focus on.

"We have to call Father," Aden said, "we need to get permission to pursuit this. He might have something else lined up,"

"Negative," Isabella said icy cold. "Father might not tell us everything but we both know our missions are our own. He never sends two of us together unless it is critical,"

"Fine," Aden said rolling his eyes and his stomach filled with butterflies at the very idea of seeing beautiful Marcus again.

Isabella got out her smartphone.

"What you searching up?" Aden asked doing the same and looking at the local media reports of the attack.

"There's only one location in the entire Canterbury area where a missile area could be launched from without the Navy getting called,"

"Impossible," Aden said before realising what she meant. "You mean this was launched from the outskirts of Canterbury,"

"And the police have already found a burnt-out truck and missile launchers have been recovered. Military grade," Isabella said.

Aden shook his head. He might have been a criminal and he had seen some amazing equipment in his family business from time to time but launching military-grade missiles, that was brave and stupid.

And this organisation clearly had money to burn.

"What are you looking up you never answered?"

"Oh sorry," Isabella asked. "I'm looking up any criminal organisation that wasn't there tonight,"

Aden had to admit that was really clever. He didn't know Isabella actually had that in her. Then he realised something he should have seen earlier.

"The crystal champagne glasses. There is only one criminal organisation in the entire underworld and international markets that only serve things in crystal.

"The Crystal Dragons," Isabella said, "and I didn't recognise anyone from that group tonight. And normally I always have a talk with Tyler,"

Aden shook his head. Tyler Cha was as fucking hot and twisted as the next serial killer but the Crystal Dragons specialised in murder, kidnapping and drugs but it was their ethical code that made Aden partly trust them.

A mass murder event was ballsy even by the Dragons standards but they had never used military-grade equipment before, they believed it only bought more trouble than it was worth.

"Where is Tyler?" Aden asked.

"London," Isabell asked. "You go up there in case you run into your Boy Toy and I'll see what my other contacts can learn in the shadows. Just be fun little brother,"

Aden hugged her and he couldn't deny that a little voice in the pit of his stomach was telling him something was extremely wrong. His sister was many things but she was never this supportive and nice to him.

She had to be working an angle and that angle terrified him a lot more than he ever wanted to admit.

CHAPTER 7
7th May 2023
London, England

Of all the reactions Marcus had expected MI5 to have last night when he eventually reported in, it definitely hadn't been a strange type of relief that most of the world's corrupt, twisted criminals and enemy intelligence officers were now dead. It wasn't exactly a weird reaction because Marcus imagined he would feel the same if he was in charge, but it still unnerved him.

Thankfully Jessica had noticed a dragon sign at the bottom of the champagne glasses used at the party, and as much as Marcus didn't want to have to deal with the Crystal Dragons because they were foul, evil murderers. He really did have to talk to them and confirm if they were behind the attack or not.

Leading him to the Dragon Pink Club in London.

Marcus leant against a warm sticky brown wall of

the club with a white towel loosely wrapped around his waist. The club was a gay sex sauna in the heart of London that specialised in serving the Leader of the Crystal Dragons, Tyler.

Marcus focused on the immense steam room he was standing in. Large columns of endless steam rose up from the floor boards, there was even a small pool in the middle of the room where two very hot young men were making out.

That was really hot to see.

The club itself was packed with tons of gay men of all different weights, heights and types. Marcus really did like looking at all the men because they were so hot and stunning to look at.

But none of them were as hot as Aden. None of these men had his natural beauty, his effortlessly fit body and his artful movements. Marcus would have loved to see him again but he doubted that was going to happen. He didn't know what he would have given up to have another kiss, another touch and just another chance to spend time with that hot man but he would have given up something.

He really, really wanted to see that beautiful man again

"Tyler," a very young man said as he walked round naked. He had to be one of the waiters "Your room is ready per your request and you have a guest,"

Marcus carefully went through the crowd of hot sexy young men around him and he went closer to where the voices were coming from.

He noticed there was a very tall Chinese man standing about ten metres from him with a golden towel wrapped around his very fit waist. He was smiling at the young man and he seemed like he was completely alone.

But Marcus wasn't stupid enough to believe that.

"Who is the guest?" Tyler asked.

"A man that did not want to be identified by his organisation only his first name is Aden," the waiter said.

Marcus shook his head. His stomach twisted into a painful knot as he realised he was finally going to see the beautiful man he wanted to do a lot of stuff to, but he couldn't get over the fact that Aden had such easy access to some of the most dangerous criminals on the planet.

Who the hell was Aden?

"That will be fine. I trust Aden and his father's organisation please tell the men to stand down," Tyler said as he went through a glass door into another steam room.

Marcus really wished he had Jessica with him so she could look at the building schematics but he had sort of looked at them earlier.

Through that door it was a long steamed corridor with a private room at the very end of it so that had to be were Aden and Tyler were meeting.

Marcus carefully glided through the crowd to get to the steamed door. He wished had a gun or something with him but he couldn't hide as much as he used to under a towel.

He went through the glass door and he was almost blinded by the sheer heat and stickiness and steam that covered his vision.

He heard footsteps come towards him.

He ducked.

A fist rushed past him.

Marcus leapt up.

Punching the guy in the chin.

He slipped.

Smashing his head on the wall.

The steam was deactivated.

The steam turned to rain.

Three men charged at him.

Marcus flew forward.

Punching one man in-between the legs.

He screamed. He fell to the floor.

Marcus jumped on his head. It cracked.

Another man kicked Marcus in the chest.

Marcus slipped.

He didn't hit his head.

The man climbed on top of Marcus.

Wrapping his hands round his throat.

Marcus punched the man's elbows.

He fell forward.

Marcus leapt up.

Climbed on him.

Snapped the man's neck.

Then Marcus stopped as he heard the cold cocking of a pistol behind him. He slowly turned around and frowned as the third man was armed and gestured Marcus to get on his knees.

Something flew through the air and the man's corpse landed with a thud a moment later.

"It seems that I have to keep saving you," Aden said at the end of the corridor. "You might want to reattach your towel before you come and join us. Very good though,"

Marcus shook his head and grinned as he realised he had lost his towel in the fight but it was good to know Aden liked his body. And now all Marcus wanted to know was what Aden's body looked like under that very short towel of his.

He really hoped he was about to find out.

CHAPTER 8
7th May 2023
London, England

Aden was so damn excited that Marcus was finally here and he had actually seen the stunning, sexy man in his full glory. Aden couldn't believe that not only was Marcus insanely fit under his clothes but he was rather nicely hung under his towel too.

He couldn't deny that he was a little nervous about his own manly parts in comparison but Aden was just glad to have the wonderful man he seriously liked joining him. And it was the perfect way to monitor what the intelligence services were doing without tipping his hand.

Aden went back into the large brown steam room where Tyler was laying butt-naked on a massage table with a small wooden table next to him filled with all sorts of scented oils, lube and condoms. Aden wasn't sure if Tyler normally got fucked every Sunday morning but he was determined to fuck him in a nonphysical way.

Tyler had information for him and Aden was more than determined to get it. There wasn't a chance in hell that Tyler was getting out of his room alive unless he helped Aden get closer to the location of Blackout.

Aden smiled as beautiful Marcus came into the steam room and he laughed a little that he was surprised to see Tyler butt-naked in front of him.

Aden went over to Tyler and gently ran a finger down his rather fit body all the way to the bottom of the spine and the associated pressure points.

Aden pressed on them.

"Ouch!" Tyler shouted.

"Now then my dear," Aden said," the Crystal Dragons attempted to assassinate me last night. We both know my father wouldn't appreciate that, and Isabella was also there,"

"We did no such thing,"

"Liar," Marcus said. "I was there too and your symbol is on all the crystal champagne glasses,"

Aden was impressed MI5 was intelligent enough to find the marking he had missed. It made him like Marcus even more if such a thing was possible.

"Fine," Tyler said. "We supplied our Crystal glasses for a Canterbury Party last night in exchange for an operation,"

"What operation?" Aden asked.

"The people we gave the supplies to. They have a lot of contacts in Russia and my mother needed an operation on her brain. There is a doctor in Russia that can do the operation. No one else I have access to can,"

Aden nodded. Tyler's mother might have been a psychotic bitch at times but if she needed a medical operation then Aden really hoped she got it.

He pressed down even harder on the pressure points. "Who did you supply the glasses to?"

"If I say then my family will disown me,"

"If you don't tell me you will die," Aden said knowing full well he would never ever kill someone unless he absolutely had to.

He looked at Marcus and he really knew Marcus was judging him but he was beautiful just standing there in that towel. So beautiful.

"Fine," Tyler said. "I only have a name and an address of a company where I personally delivered the glasses to. Olav Redstone of Olav Exports,"

Marcus laughed. "You're kidding, right?"

Aden grabbed some of the scented oils and poured them all over Tyler's back and he moaned in pleasure. Aden was actually surprised the oils were warm for a change. This place really was professional.

Aden made a Lighter sound to scare Tyler, he loved it how Marcus was forcing himself not to laugh.

"Don't," Tyler said like a little girl. "I'm not kidding,"

"What's wrong?" Aden asked.

"Olav Exports is a major international front with billions of pounds of investment in the UK," Marcus said.

"Good so you can siege their accounts," Aden said.

"No. According to the Government the UK relies too much on the investment for us to siege it but at least we have a name," Marcus said.

Tyler kicked Aden.

He fell backwards.

Tyler pushed up.

Whipping out a pistol.

Marcus flew forward.

Punching Tyler in the jaw.

Aden ran forward.

Kicking Tyler in the jaw.

Tyler was out cold but Aden didn't want to leave a criminal leader that tried to kill them both breathing. His father had taught him a lot over the years and one of his biggest lessons was that if an enemy leaves alive then they will come after you again and again until one of you is dead.

Aden looked at the various scented oils and other massage chemicals on the little table and he picked them up. They were all toxic if swallowed so he poured them all into Tyler's mouth and nose and just left him there to die.

As him and Marcus left the room he made sure that Marcus left first in case he had the stupid idea to try and save Tyler without him knowing.

Aden led them down the long corridor back out into the main steam room. "It looks like we're working together now,"

"Really?" Marcus asked laughing. "I'm a government official. You're a criminal. We don't work together,"

"That might be true in normal times but you have government resources and I have my criminal network. And I am sure your government wants Blackout back as much as I do?"

"What's in it for you?"

Aden grinned because he really did hate lying to such a kind, beautiful and cute man but he was going to have to.

"I get to spend a little more time with you,"

"And I know that isn't it but I trust you wouldn't kill me for now,"

"Try ever," Aden said meaning every single word of it.

Aden held the door open for Marcus and now he couldn't believe he was finally working with a beautiful man from MI5 that he would have to deal with at some point. But he meant what he said, *he* would never kill Marcus and he seriously hoped he could keep the rest of his family from doing the same.

An impossible wish if there ever was one.

CHAPTER 9
7th May 2023
London, England

As much as Marcus never ever intended to take sexy Aden back to MI5, he was perfectly okay taking him to the small MI5 safe house that him and Jessica had been using as their unofficial base of operations for a little while and it was the perfect place to hopefully get some prints off Aden.

Not that he believed Aden was stupid enough to fall for any of their tricks for a moment.

Marcus led hot as hell Aden into their little London apartment with great views overlooking all the top London landmarks and the River Thames as it swirled, twirled and churned around itself. Marcus really liked that Jessica had cleaned the apartment a lot so even the dark wooden floors shone a little and the bright white cabinets and walls dazzled in the late morning sun.

There was even three piping hot mugs of coffee

on the round dining table for them to enjoy but Marcus didn't like it how Jessica's computer was running and she wasn't about.

Then the toilet flushed and Jessica came out behind them and went back over to her computer. Marcus had to admit she looked great with her shortish blond hair that was a little messy but done in a really stylish way and her slim-fitting black dress made her look great.

He still couldn't believe she didn't have a boyfriend. A lot of men were seriously missing out.

"Nice you finally joined us," Jessica said as she stood up again and offered Aden a hug.

Aden laughed. "Oh cool you're holding a pin-tracking device on your index finger of your left hand. Is that the old version or the newer version with a 200-metre listening capability?"

Marcus just laughed because he was seriously starting to fall for Aden. He was smart, beautiful and he seemed to know everything.

"Maybe the newer version," Jessica said like a child that had just been told off so she put it down and offered the hug again.

Aden smiled. "If we're going to hug then get rid of the two small listening devices on your left arm that come off the moment they touch my clothes. There is another small red dot on your dress that is something. And I don't doubt there is something else you're hiding,"

"Can we please keep him? He is amazing,"

Jessica asked.

Marcus laughed because he would have been perfectly happy keeping such a sexy man with him at all times. But he was surprised and rather impressed that Aden knew so much about spyware and whatnot. It wasn't normal to know *this* much, so he couldn't workout what exactly Aden's family was in to.

"What have you got on Olav Exports?" Marcus asked.

Jessica sat down at her computer. "Three main offices in Europe, the UK and Asia. Olav himself has been connected to over three hundred deaths and assassination attempts and there is even evidence he's murdered entire villages in Asia so he could expand his poppy farm,"

"He's a drug dealer," Marcus said.

"Exactly," Jessica said, "but he came to the attention of MI5 last year when he killed two of our officers in broad daylight after Border Force captured three million pounds worth of Heroin entering the country. And he funds three main terrorist organisations that focus on the UK,"

Marcus shook his head. They really needed to take Olav out and destroy his entire network all over the world but sadly that wasn't his job as an MI5 officer. His job was just to protect the UK no matter the cost.

"Why does he want Blackout then?" Aden asked.

"I don't know," Marcus said. "It doesn't seem normal for him to want something that… oh,"

Marcus couldn't believe he had been so stupid because he now understood exactly why Olav wanted Blackout. If he was that annoyed at Border Force for stopping his Heroin getting into the country then the easiest way to get revenge would be to knockout the UK's entire power network including their secure systems.

Meaning Olav could literally just fly the Heroin in without it even being registered and Olav definitely had the means to get missiles for the attack on the Hall. A simple flight during a blackout would be easy for the likes of him.

So Marcus told Aden and Jessica all of this.

"Bring up a chair kids," Jessica said smiling and grabbing her cup of coffee. "We have to do some research and we have to find Olav before he strikes,"

Marcus couldn't agree more and he just grinned as Aden picked up the coffee mug. Maybe he would know exactly who the hot sexy man was sooner than he ever thought possible.

Little did Marcus realise he was going to have the shock of his life the moment he found out.

CHAPTER 10
7th May 2023
London, England

Aden was flat out impressed that an organisation as poorly run, smelly and almost pointless as MI5 could actually afford a safehouse or safe-apartment as nice as this one. This was a lot better with its great views, cleanliness and good white cabinets compared to the one him and Isabella had stayed in last night.

It was just impressive.

Aden rather liked sitting at the dining table with Jessica typing around on her computer, each key press making a tapping sound that echoed off the smooth walls of the apartment. And it was really cosy with the warming, bitter hints of coffee filling the air.

Aden could hardly judge Marcus for wanting to use the cup for his fingerprints but MI5 wouldn't find anything or even if they did everything would done be by the time they found out who his father was and what items he might have given to his father in the past.

He was running a search through his various criminal social media groups about if anyone had seen Olav in recent days and if anyone wanted to kill him. It might have been a risky move but he had to prove to Marcus that he was serious about finding Olav and seriously about how cute he was.

Marcus was just sitting at the table too with one leg over the other humming lightly to himself a merry little tune that Aden didn't recognise. It was rather sweet seeing Marcus relaxed for a change as he too ran a search.

"What you know Jess?" Marcus asked.

"Not very well. I've running Olav through every single private and public camera in the entire UK to find him,"

"Is that legal?" Aden asked not knowing why he cared.

"Nope because we technically need a warrant to search through private footage but what the UK public doesn't know won't hurt them,"

Aden smiled because that was such a lie. The UK Public doesn't know that Blackout could be used to knock out every single electronic product in the entire country and that would hurt them a lot.

"I'm out of leads," Marcus said. "Looks like it's all down to you Jess,"

Aden had no idea why Marcus didn't believe in him and his sources but he really wanted to spend a little bit of time just getting to know what Marcus was like, what was his past and why did he do what he did.

And he really just wanted an excuse to talk to him, he was so cute today.

"How did you join the Service?" Aden asked.

Marcus smiled and looked at Jess who nodded, Aden found that a little weird. Maybe Jessica was his boss or more senior than him or maybe it was a sign that Marcus wanted Jessica to be careful in case Aden was searching for information. Whatever it was Aden knew he had to be very, very careful here.

"About five years ago when I was 18 my mother and father died in a car crash. It wasn't anything that normal because the van driver was a terrorist who was escaping from driving into a high street filled with people,"

Aden reached for Marcus's hand out of instinct and he was so glad he let him take it. He really liked how warm, smooth and nice it felt to hold Marcus's hands in his own.

"I'm so sorry," Aden said, "I didn't know but it's a pain losing family. I was abandoned when I was a kid barely ten years old so my now-father found me and loved me,"

"And made you into a criminal," Jessica said.

"I simply get items for him. Whatever he does with the items is his business," Aden said firmly and he really didn't understand why MI5 was so interested in *his* history when they had Olav to deal with.

"Did you never really know your parents?" Marcus asked.

Aden was about to answer when he realised how caringly, lovingly and kindly he had asked. No one had ever said something that nice to him before and no one, besides his father, had cared enough about him to ask.

That only made Aden like Marcus even more. He was so perfect.

"I still have some memories of them and they did love me a lot. I don't really know why they abandoned me and I still look them up online at times. They're successful bankers in London now worth millions of pounds,"

"Oh,"

Aden held Marcus's hands even tighter. "It's okay. I have a comfortable, good life with a family that loves me,"

"If they loved you then why are you alone?" Jessica asked as she typed more on her laptop.

Aden forced himself to relax. He really didn't want her or Marcus suspecting that Isabella wasn't watching his every move, she was actually one of the people he was waiting to reply.

As soon as Isabella or his father contacted him Aden knew that it would be all systems go and then his father and his forces would descend on Olav's location *after* they were there so he could just take Blackout without Aden having to steal it from MI5.

He just wanted Marcus to be kept safe. That was his only concern.

"I am more than capable of looking after

myself," Aden said hoping that be enough for Jessica.

"Fair enough," Marcus said. "Do you have a boyfriend?"

"Enough," Jessica said. And Aden finally realised exactly what that nod had been about earlier, it was good to know Marcus was more than interested in him and he had been concerned he might tell Aden too much.

Hence why Jessica had to make sure he was behaving himself.

Aden kissed Marcus's hands and grinned as Isabella texted him back with a location for Olav. So he wiped his fingerprints off the mug and was looking forward to telling Marcus where they were going.

"He's at a farmhouse in Yorkshire," Aden said. "I'll send you the address now,"

"Wait," Jessica said standing up. "How can we trust you and your source?"

"You don't have an option unless you have better information," Aden said coldly.

Aden loved it as Jessica frowned and nodded and Aden knew that everything was going to plan.

But his stomach tightened into a painful knot as he realised his hope and dream of making sure Marcus didn't get hurt might be a lot harder than he ever thought possible.

Especially with Isabella watching his every move.

CHAPTER 11
7th May 2023
Yorkshire, England

As the fiery sun started to set and set the sky ablaze in a firestorm of red, pink and orange, Marcus leant on the cold flint wall of the property in his full tactical gear.

He was really impressed with the tall green hills all around him that were thankfully clear of enemies and he was pleased that Olav's security seemed to be third-world at best because he couldn't see any guards about.

Out in front of him was a few hundred metres of long thick green grass that probably would have come up to Marcus's knees and led towards a massive brown farmhouse like it had been picked up from the American South and just landed in Yorkshire like it had been transported by aliens. There were no clear signs of security, no cameras and no signs of life except for the lights were on in the house.

None of this made any sense but judging by the road markings and the tyre tracks on the road, Marcus didn't doubt there had been a lot of movement lately. They had either just missed them completely or something else was happening.

Marcus took out his two Glocks and smiled as beautiful, sexy Aden took out his knives. He almost couldn't believe he had almost asked if Aden had a boyfriend or not but he really, really wanted to know.

In this line of work it was just impossible to meet men as beautiful, hot and sexy as Aden and Marcus didn't want to leave him at the end of this mission. He felt a strange connection to Aden that went way beyond attraction, it was nice talking to him and learning about him and his past.

And it only made Marcus fall in love with him even more.

"Come in," Jessica said over his earpiece.

"We're here," Marcus said. "No signs of life. Does the satellite have anything?"

"Sort of. It seems there are life signs in the farmhouse maybe ten guys so be careful. I would recommend waiting until dark,"

Marcus was surprised that Aden looked a little panicked by that realisation but he didn't blame him. There was nowhere near to rest and watch the farmhouse except for this stretch of road. And each moment they were out here the greater chance there was of being discovered.

This wasn't ideal.

"We're going to breach now," Marcus said.

"Confirmed," Jessica said. "And Aria wants me to remind you that Blackout is the prize here. Nothing else matters,"

"Okay," Marcus said looking at the beautiful man standing next to him.

"Let's go," Aden said.

Marcus hopped over the flint wall and couldn't believe that he had jumped straight into a pile of cow shit and seriously didn't smell grand.

Aden laughed and Marcus shook his head as they crouched down low to blend into the grass and they went towards the farmhouse.

The key for these sorts of missions was to always be silent, careful and completely aware of the surroundings. Marcus hated hearing stories about his friends being killed because they didn't see a landmine or a guard opening the door.

Marcus kept going forward.

It was even worse on this mission because all Marcus wanted to do was keep Aden safe. He wanted to date him so he couldn't date a corpse.

Marcus noticed a door was opening up ahead that led out onto a patio area.

Marcus stopped immediately and ducked into the long thick grass. There was a tall woman in a white business blouse, trainers and trousers. She lit up a smoke.

He looked at Aden close behind him and he shook his head Aden was already lining up one of his knives to kill her.

Marcus wasn't completely against it but they did have a mission to do. Each death would only increase the risk of detection.

"Hello?" the woman asked.

Marcus looked at the woman and was so relieved she was on the phone to someone and she was distracted.

He gestured they continue on and make sure that they weren't seen. He was still impressed as hell at how artful, elegant and stunning Aden was as he moved through the entire grass field without making a single sound.

Marcus really couldn't imagine doing the same.

When they were on the very edge of the long thick grass Marcus stopped and the woman was still standing there on her phone just clicking through stuff. She was still distracted but she wasn't talking to anyone.

Marcus hated it as Aden whistled and the woman came over.

Then like an angel of death Aden grabbed the woman and killed her before she could even register what was happening.

Marcus smiled when he noticed the woman was carrying a lot of knives herself. She was a guard and at least they had just given themselves one less enemy to deal with.

They both stood up and went over to the glass door the woman had walked out of and it was open.

Marcus went inside and he really hoped that this mission wasn't going to be something he was going to regret.

Little did Marcus realise his entire world was about to be turned upside down and not for the reasons he ever expected.

GAY ROMANCE COLLECTION VOLUME 4

CHAPTER 12
7th May 2023
Yorkshire, England

Aden really hadn't wanted to kill that female guard but he seriously wanted this entire affair to just hurry up now because sooner or later his father would be here and he needed that damn Blackout to make sure he didn't fail his father.

It was that simple.

As him and Marcus went through the glass door, he made sure his knives were ready to strike and that he was aware of the three opened doors ahead. They slowly went up the long brown wooden corridor that stuck of cat wee but Aden hadn't heard a cat here so that was always a good sign.

Aden looked in the first door and that was just a small kitchen area that was empty. That was good.

Aden watched as Marcus looked through another door and that was empty and then they both heard the sound of a TV turning on coming from the direction of the third door.

Aden nodded to Marcus to tell him they would storm in there together and thankfully Marcus understood the sign.

They stormed in.

The room was completely empty besides from an armchair, a TV and a webcam that was very much focused on them.

Aden threw a knife at the TV to turn it off and then he threw another at the webcam for good measure. He got the knives back with a simple flick of his wrist.

There was no other way in or out of the room so it made no sense that someone had turned on the TV and managed to escape before they had got there.

Aden went over to one of the long rough block walls and noticed there was a bookcase right in front of where the door would logically be located. He checked the floor and noticed there were cuts in the floor so the bookcase should have swung out.

Marcus held his ear and Aden shook his head as he hated that Jessica was talking to him and for some reason he wasn't able to hear it this time. He really hoped that geeky woman hadn't managed to figure out who his father was.

Not that it mattered because soon he would have Blackout, a proud father and a very safe Marcus. That was all he wanted.

Aden gestured Marcus to come and help him move the bookcase.

"What was that about?" Aden asked quietly as Marcus came over to help him.

"Nothing much just that Jessica noticed a heat signature in the surrounding hills. Maybe a guard or something,"

Aden forced himself not to react. That was probably Isabella finally arriving after being delayed by their father for hours. If she was here as the vanguard then his father and his forces would be here soon.

Aden was running out of time.

They pulled the case with a massive pull and the bookcase swung open and a lot of voices started to become a lot louder.

Marcus fired.

Bullets firing into flesh.

Aden flew at them.

Knives slicing through flesh.

Blood sprayed up walls.

Corpses bleed on the ground.

Painting the floors.

Aden smiled as he looked at his handy work. These idiots never saw what was coming. No one moved on the other side. There were no voices, no sounds of movement and not even any sounds of breathing.

Aden went through to the room the bookcase had been blocking and he carefully poked his head round the edge of the bookcase and there were only three tall men in tight sexy black suits pointing their weapons at his head and Olav was sitting on a sofa like he was in total control of the situation.

Then Aden heard ten more men come in behind them and he just couldn't believe they had been completely outflanked and now they were surrounded.

"Come out from your bookcase," a guard said.

Aden looked at the beautiful man he really wanted to protect more than anything and Marcus nodded at him. Aden still made sure his knives could be thrown the moment they needed to be but he lowered them just enough that an untrained person might stupidly believe they were safe.

"Now then," Olav said in a perfect English accent, "we have a lot to discuss including how the hell the son of a criminal mastermind and an MI5 Officer found me,"

As much as Aden wanted Marcus to be spared of this conversation he knew it was flat out impossible and he had no idea if him or Marcus would be walking out of here alive.

No idea at all.

CHAPTER 13
7th May 2023
Yorkshire, England

Marcus wanted nothing more than to simply shoot all these idiots in the head as they dared to threaten the beautiful man he seriously liked. Marcus was forced to throw his gun over to Olav and then he felt the cold metal barrel of a gun against the back of his head.

He watched as the foul monsters placed another gun barrel at the back of Aden's head too.

All Marcus wanted to do was charge at that particular guard and kill him. It was only now that he was realising how much he liked and wanted to protect to Aden. The mission didn't matter only the sweet, kind man that he almost loved mattered.

"How is your father these days?" Olav asked.

Marcus had no idea who Aden's father was or why the hell he was so well-known but he really wanted to find out. He hoped that Jessica had found something back at the safe house but he doubted it. Aden seemed to be way too smart to leave anything behind.

"Very well thank you," Aden said. "However he is greatly hurt that you have such an item that he is after,"

"Then your father should have spoken to me himself instead of teaming up with this goodie scumbag,"

Marcus laughed. He had been called a lot in his time but that certainly had to be a new one. He looked at the three men next to Olav they were starting to relax now and that made him question why didn't they think Aden was going to kill them and their Master.

"Who is your father?" Marcus asked.

He realised he should have asked that a hell of a lot earlier but maybe Jessica was right maybe he had been too focused on Aden's beauty.

Olav started laughing. Marcus noticed the men were looking uneasily at each other and even the guard behind him dug the gun a little more into his skull.

They clearly weren't used to their boss laughing. And Marcus wasn't sure if that was good or bad.

There wasn't a clear way out of the situation just yet so he needed to do two things. Stay alive long enough to find an escape route and try to find out as much information as possible.

"Jessica," Marcus said quietly in case his earpiece

was still working but he hated how quiet Jessica had been for the last few minutes.

"Don't talk. I'm still here. I can see that you have 13 foes and Olav keeping you at gun point and remember there is that woman in the hills too. Maybe she's another foe,"

Marcus rolled his eyes. This seriously wasn't good news.

"I'll try to get you backup but that won't be for another half an hour,"

All Marcus wanted was some good news and it was just typical that Jessica only ever gave him bad news.

"Why do you want Blackout?" Marcus asked gesturing he wanted to come forward and thankfully Olav let him.

It was even better when the man with the gun in the back of his head didn't follow him. Marcus could start thinking up a way to escape hopefully.

"Blackout is the future of mass casualty warfare," Olav said. "Sure bombs, missiles and suicide bombers are highly effective weapons for mass destruction but, I ask you this MI5, why should I use weapons against a society when I can simply cause a society to kill itself?"

Marcus didn't understand exactly what he meant for a few moments. Then he realised just how twisted and stupid Olav really was.

"You mean to tell me that if you knocked out a country's or a good few of them and their electronic systems. Then security, computer and military systems will be down," Marcus said. "That would cause mass destruction, robbery and violence,"

"And better yet," Olav said. "Heads of State like Russia and China and Iran will be paying me handsomely to knock out the systems of their neighbours. The Russian Empire will be reborn and the New Russian Empire will eclipse the old one,"

"You're insane," Aden said.

Marcus couldn't agree more.

"You two are fools as is your father Aden,"

"Incoming," Jessica said through the earpiece.

Marcus looked at Aden. "You might need to duck,"

A missile screamed through the air.

Marcus and Aden leapt to one side.

Marcus tackled a guard to the ground.

A missile struck the farmhouse.

A wall exploded.

Sending deadly shards into the guards.

A helicopter landed outside.

Marcus punched the guard.

Killing him.

Marcus ripped the gun off his corpse and leapt up.

Six guards got up.

Marcus fired.

He charged.

Aden threw his knives.

They smashed into chests.

Blood poured out of them.

Guards screamed.

Marcus looked around for Olav.

He started to run away.

Marcus shot him in the knee.

And when Marcus went over to see him he saw exactly what he wanted, on Olav's bloody right wrist was Blackout or at least the command part of the larger system.

Marcus took it off his wrist and grinned. He was surprised that such a tiny watch-like device could destroy entire countries and bring down governments and usher in a brand-new age of tyranny. He was almost tempted to annihilate it there and then to make sure that no one could ever use it.

But he had his orders and he had to get this back to MI5 before something bad happened.

"Wow," Aden said, "that's Blackout. Can I hold it?"

Marcus just grinned at the beautiful man. Aden was so cute and sweet and clever as he stood there smiling. Marcus really couldn't have done this without him and as Olav started laughing next to him, Marcus nodded and passed him Blackout.

It wasn't like Aden was going to run off with it, use it or actually do anything with it. Marcus trusted Aden and after the chaos of the past two days he didn't doubt that Aden would ever betray him.

"Excellent work little brother," a woman said.

Marcus jumped as the woman from the hall went

over to Aden and hugged him tight.

    What the fuck was happening?

    He had killed her. Surely?

CHAPTER 14
7th May 2023
Yorkshire, England

Aden absolutely hated the entire damn situation as he felt Isabella's wonderfully warm arms around him. There were still little pieces of ash floating down and some of the farmhouse on the other side was on fire and the smell of smoke and charred flesh filled the air.

Aden hated seeing Marcus's look of horror form on his beautiful face as he realised what was happening. Aden had never wanted this to happen or anything else, he had only ever wanted to protect, save and maybe even love Marcus a little bit.

It was clear that was never ever going to happen and it was all his fault. At least this would now be the end and Marcus wouldn't have to see him again.

"What does it feel like?" Isabella asked like a kid in a candy store.

Aden rubbed the perfectly smooth black metal of

the watch in his hands and it felt good and really nice. He felt powerful, rich and like he could do anything. Mostly he was just glad that his father would be proud of him but holding Blackout did make him feel good.

"My turn little brother," Isabella said.

"Was this the plan all along?" Marcus asked.

Aden shook his head. "I did this to protect you actually,"

"My son really did do it all to save you," a man said with a deep, booming voice.

Aden jumped at the sound of his father and his stomach tightened into a painful knot. He really hoped his father was proud of him and that nothing bad was going to happen.

"Count Harrad of the Crimson Gauntlet Crime Family," Marcus said. "Responsible for the murder of fifty people, the sales of tens of millions of pounds' worth of black market weaponry and so many more crimes I don't know where to start,"

Aden shrugged. He wasn't that bothered by what other business arrangements his father got up to because his father loved him more than his real parents ever had. His father was a good man, a questionable man at times but he was a good man at heart.

His father came over and took Blackout from Isabella and he kissed *her* of all people on the head and not him.

"I got Blackout for you father," Aden said like a

child.

"I know," his father said getting out his characteristic golden gun and pointing it at Marcus.

"Wait," Aden said. "Father we cannot kill him. We have to escape now and make sure that MI5 don't track us,"

Aden really had no damn idea why his father wanted to be such an idiot about this. They couldn't kill Marcus, he was such a good person, such a beautiful man and Aden didn't want to live in a world without him even if they weren't dating.

"Can I please kill him dad?" Isabella asked. "I can make it painful, like super painful,"

Aden looked at Marcus and he could see the shock, the betrayal and the sheer look of horror in his eyes. He hated that Marcus had to see this and experience it.

He wasn't sure how to protect the man that he wanted to fuck so badly besides from doing the extreme, but maybe that was the only way to save Marcus. And maybe bring down his father at the same time.

Aden shook the stupid idea away because he just couldn't betray his father. His father was totally a good man at heart, he was loving and Aden forced himself to think of another lie.

He just didn't want his father to kill Marcus.

"Let's take him with us," Aden said. "He's an MI5 Intelligence officer inside his head is a whole bunch of state secrets that we can sell to our friends, his enemies,"

Aden subtly winked at Marcus but he had no idea if Marcus knew he was doing this out of some twisted love. Marcus probably didn't because intelligence officers could be so thick at times.

"Sure," his father said. "I have the Head of the Russian Federal Security Services arriving tomorrow morning anyway. We can hand him over then as well for extra resources,"

Aden didn't know how much better any of this was but it proved that Marcus might live to see another day.

"Come on," his father said. "We're going back to the chopper before MI5 shows up. Make sure our guest is knocked out and alive for now,"

Aden smiled as a guard knocked out Marcus and he was so relieved that Marcus was alive.

Then Isabella came so close to him that Aden could feel her breathe on his ear. "But just remember that I love killing at night and whenever I fancy it. I wonder how long your boyfriend will last before I go cut, slice and bang on him,"

Aden forced out a laugh because that was what she was expecting but now Aden realised he absolutely had to save the man he loved.

And sadly he did actually love Marcus, as annoying as that realisation was.

CHAPTER 15
8th May 2023
Unknown Location, United Kingdom or Rest of World

The thick smells of petrol, burning rubber and charred flesh filled the air as Marcus finally woke up. He had no idea how long he had been out, he didn't know where he was and now all he wanted in the entire world was to know what the hell had just happened.

He flat out couldn't believe that Aden had betrayed him so badly. And he had been stupid enough to let that little traitor into his mind, heart and soul.

Marcus took a long deep breath of the awful air and made himself focus on his surroundings. He could focus on the bloody traitor later but for now he just had to survive. The UK was doomed if he distracted himself for too long.

The pitch darkness of wherever he was might

have limited what he could see but Marcus was more than glad he had been in dark places before. His other senses became heightened and they allowed him to focus more on other features of the environment.

There was a loud deafening hum and bang and pop all around him but it seemed to be focused behind him. Marcus recognised the little sound from his days exploring ferries with his brother when they should have been above deck.

Marcus loved getting into trouble with Ryan.

He wasn't sure why he was on a ship or ferry but that would make sense. It would certainly explain why no one had never managed to find Harrald's base of operations.

It was because it was always moving from one city to another city via the oceans and sea. Damn Harrald and his criminal family.

Marcus tried to move his fingers slightly but he couldn't. They felt tied to something and the rough texture told him that he was *only* bound with thick rough rope that dug into his wrists the more he struggled.

He knew he shouldn't have been surprised at all by the skill of Harald's men and women but he still was. He was more surprised that such a brilliant and sexy man like Aden was working with him but that was just an annoying detail.

Marcus tried to find the knot but he couldn't.

He tried to move his feet but they tied even tighter onto the chair and he wasn't even sure that was correct. He only knew he was tied onto something cold, hard and something that didn't allow him to move.

The lights exploded on.

Marcus closed his eyes for a brief moment as his eyes adjusted to the bright white light all around him. Why couldn't criminals just have nice dim lights for their guests? It was so damn rude of them.

Marcus shook his head as he saw that Isabella woman walk towards him in-between the tall metal crates filled with guns, bombs and other weapons if their labels were to be believed. He doubted it but still.

He supposed Isabella wasn't a bad looking woman in her black military gear but it was her eyes that concerned him. They were hungry, deranged and they were looking at Marcus like how he used to look at twinks when he was a new outed man that wanted to experience all the pleasures of gay society.

He had both loved and hated his whore era in equal measure despite how sensational the sex was.

"My little brother likes you a lot," Isabella said taking out a knife.

"He is hot," Marcus said wanting to buy himself as much time as possible to escape. He didn't know why but he seriously had a sense that Aden was going to save him at some point but until then Marcus had to try to save himself.

"Do you love him?"

"I don't know. I've always found that word a

little hard to say myself. What about you Isabella, have you ever loved someone?"

"Of course," she said scratching the edge of the knife against a metal crate. "I have loved many, many men and then I have killed them all. I am very much a one night stand sort of girl,"

"More like a one-night kill sort of girl," Marcus said grinning.

Isabella clapped. "Oh you are a goodie. I will enjoy killing you. How about we start with a chopped finger or something? Maybe even a little toe,"

"I thought your father said to keep me alive and intact for the FSB coming later on," Marcus said. "Would you really want to disobey your father?"

"My father will be dead soon anyway and once I have killed him then everything will be mine and everything you have come to love will be burnt to the ground," Isabella said smiling.

Marcus gulped because he might have had a way to destroy this organisation from the inside but he needed someone on his side. He doubted that Aden would do anything that might cause a conflict between him and Isabella even if it meant keeping his father alive.

Marcus really needed to escape sooner rather than later and warn Aden. There was about to be a civil war within this organisation and Marcus really didn't want Aden to suffer.

Even though that was basically impossible at this point.

"Isabella return to the bridge," a man said.

Marcus smiled at her. "When you return at least have the decency to fight me in a combat before you start hacking me up,"

Isabella gave him a little bow and then she went away.

Marcus started pulling harder and harder on the ropes because he seriously needed to be free before she got back.

Otherwise the idea of him letting Aden suffer in this civil war scared him a lot more than he ever wanted to admit.

CHAPTER 16
8th May 2023

Twenty Miles Off The English Coast

Aden seriously hated himself as he leant against the icy coldness of the metal walls of the square bridge as he waited for Isabella of all people to join them in the Bridge. The white sterile walls reflected the bright white lights of the bridge perfectly and only made it seem brighter compared to the sheer darkness of the world outside.

Aden could barely see where the black water started and the pitch darkness of the sky stopped. It was that dark outside and with the five women in their blue uniforms wiping the sleep from their eyes, Aden couldn't blame them for feeling so tired.

He had managed to grab some sleep earlier in the evening but he hadn't really slept too much. He felt so guilty about Marcus and everything that was happening and he was seriously starting to doubt the sheer wisdom of his father.

Aden had always known his father was a sort of bad man but he could see and hear the sheer anger and rage in Marcus' voice about the crimes his father had facilitated. All those innocent lives lost, but still his father couldn't be that bad considering he had raised him when no one else wanted him?

He shook the silly thought away and looked at his father in his full-captain uniform that made him look like a military officer for a moment. His father was leaning against a wooden table filled with maps and whatnot about their current destination.

Then Blackout was on his wrist.

"How does it work Dad?" Aden asked.

Aden loved it as his father smiled how Aden liked to imagine a loving father would grin at his son when he made them extra proud.

"Simple son," his Father said as he gestured him over to his side and pointed to all the dials and buttons on the watch-like device. "You simply click this button to activate it and then you keep moving the dials until they lock onto the Satellite network that Blackout runs on,"

"Then you simply programme Blackout to hit an area and then the world burns," Isabella said as she came in.

Aden hated how his Father immediately started hugging Isabella instead of him. All Aden wanted was a nice friendly hug from his father but clearly that was never going to happen.

"Here's the woman of the hour," his father said.

"This is the woman that made all of this possible,"

Isabella grinned. "Thank you. It wasn't easy having to suggest and escort Aden round like a little dog but I managed to train him,"

"You see son if you keep learning from your sister you will rule this organisation one day instead of her,"

Aden took a few steps back when he saw the sheer rage and anger in her eyes. And Aden realised that Isabella wanted him dead. She didn't love him, she didn't like him, she didn't even value him.

His corpse was all she had ever wanted.

"Father get away from her," Aden said getting out one of his knives.

The female crew in the bridge stood up and aimed his pistols at him.

"What's going on?" his Father said.

But it was too late.

A shot went off and the bullet screamed through his Father's chest and his Father's corpse slumped to the ground.

Then all the women focused their weapons on Aden and Isabella started laughing.

"I actually didn't intend to do all this for another year but Blackout gives me such an opportunity. I could have the likes of the West, China and Russia all bow down to me like a Goddess,"

"You're crazy," Aden said.

"Of course I am but I am a crazy woman with a weapon capable of rebuilding the world in my image.

Once I knock out the West's electronic systems then China will march. And then I will be the Ruler or a Governor in the New Chinese Empire,"

Aden shook his head. Not only because of the sheer craziness of his sister's words but because he actually believed them. He knew that Isabella was a soft mark for anyone clever enough to find the right lie and then Aden realised that his entire life had been a lie too.

His father had never loved him. He had been homeless, desperate and lonely on the streets so whenever anyone would come and show him the smallest amount of kindness he would be all over them.

Aden supposed it had never been hard for Harald to groom him and make him one of his sons just like all the other vulnerable people in the organisation.

"What now?" Aden asked.

Isabella grinned. "Crew turn this ship around and when the FSB chopper gets within range shoot it down and make sure it looks like the West did it,"

"No," Aden said. "That's insane. If Russia and China believe the West assassinated the head of their intelligence service then it could easily start World War Three,"

"Exactly. Then coupled with the Blackout on the West that will happen a few hours later it will simply look like the East is taking revenge. And then World War Three will start and the West will lose,"

"Bastard," Aden said.

"Because we have had some good times together little brother I will give you ten minutes and hide and then I will hunt you down. And kill you,"

"You know exactly where I'm going,"

Isabella just grinned. "Tick tock little mouse,"

Aden ran out the Bridge and seriously hoped he could get Marcus to help save him before they were killed.

And the fate of the world was doomed.

CHAPTER 17
8th May 2023

Twenty-Two Miles Off The English Coast

Marcus had to admit whoever tied these knots were flat out amazing because he could not get out of these knots at all. He had already felt the ship move so something was clearly happening and that only made him want to escape even more.

The heavy metal door to the room opened and Marcus's eyes widened when he saw beautiful sexy Aden run towards him with his knives out.

"Hello traitor," Marcus said without meaning to.

Aden didn't talk as he cut Marcus free and normally if it was anyone else he would have punched, kicked and got the man in a headlock. But he forced himself not to.

Aden might have been a traitor but Marcus didn't doubt there was a good reason for all of it.

"I know I have no right to ask this but I need your help,"

"Three words," Marcus said.

"Isabella in charge. World War Three. Blackout being used,"

Marcus rolled his eyes. It wasn't exactly three words but he would take it because if that psychotic bitch was in charge then something had gone seriously wrong.

And they had to stop it.

Marcus went over to the metal crates all around him and opened them. They were all empty and Marcus supposed that was fair. It would have been a little stupid leaving him with crates full of weapons.

A man exploded through the door.

He fired his gun.

Marcus jumped behind some crates.

Aden threw a knife.

And as the man went down Marcus went straight over to him and picked up the idiot's weapon. He didn't have a lot of shots left but Marcus just wanted to survive.

All whilst keeping Aden safe at the same time.

"We have to kill Isabella," Marcus said, "and get Blackout back,"

"No," Aden said. "Blackout is too powerful for any country or power to have. We have to make sure Blackout is destroyed forever,"

Marcus hated the idea of that. His bosses were going to be so annoyed but he just focused on Aden's soft beautiful lips and realised he might be right.

He touched his earpiece and hoped beyond hope

that Jessica was still there.

"Come in Jessica," Marcus said.

A small amount of static filled his ear so there was still a signal but it was too weak to broadcast.

"We have to get to higher ground then we can call in a naval strike," Marcus said, "and get rid of this ship forever,"

Aden nodded.

A woman stormed in.

Marcus shot the woman in the head.

He gestured they needed to go now because they were sitting ducks in this room.

Marcus opened the heavy metal door and made sure the little metal ship corridor was clean. For a change it was.

He led him and Aden out of the room and from what he knew about ships they needed to turn left and keep going forward.

Marcus kept his gun level in front of him and his wrist relaxed as they went forward. He checked each door and made sure that no one was following them.

No one was.

There was a metal staircase up ahead. A perfect ambush site then Marcus realised the ceiling had turned into a metal grate that allowed him to see who was above them and it made them easier to see.

Bullets screamed down from above.

Marcus jumped forward.

He spun around.

Shooting straight up.

Two corpses fell to the ground.

Marcus hurried up and led Aden up a staircase and onto another deck. The static in his ear was getting a little louder but it still wasn't good enough to broadcast.

"Stop!" a woman shouted.

Aden threw a knife into her neck and retrieved it as they moved past the corpse.

Marcus was really pleased he was with him. They turned around two corners and went into a massive dining hall and then the entire crew stood up, aimed their guns at them and Marcus just laughed.

"You could have warned me," he said to Aden.

"I haven't been on his ship in months. I forget,"

And as much as Marcus wanted to believe that this was just yet another case of Aden betraying him he really knew that this wasn't.

All the crew came over to them and took their guns and knives and escorted them to the bridge.

And Marcus just grinned because that would mean there would be less interference with the earpiece and now Marcus was hoping beyond hope he could contact Jessica.

At least in time to save the world.

CHAPTER 18

8th May 2023

Ten Miles off The Coast Of France

Aden seriously hated how the icy coldness of the gun barrel was being rammed into his back as the dumb crew escorted him and beautiful Marcus into the Bridge. He wasn't even sure why Isabella of all people wanted them alive but at least it gave them another shot to escape.

"I didn't want them here," Isabella said as she hunched herself over the wooden table filled with charts and maps and all sorts of other wonders that Aden would have been more happy burning.

Anything if it meant Isabella would suffer.

Aden looked at Marcus and noticed he was focusing on something. He knew he still had his earpiece but Aden wasn't sure how it worked and would the sign even be picked up this far off the English coast.

He really hoped it was.

Aden looked at the three female crew members that were controlling the ship and doing all sorts of things Aden didn't understand. But he knew they were the key, if he could only damage the controls then maybe that would stop Isabella from doing something.

Or maybe that would destroy the ship and Blackout with it.

"But we did want them here," the crew said.

Aden was surprised when the crew member took the gun out of his back and pointed it at Isabella. A few other people gasped.

Aden had no idea how far the corruption and turncoats spread but it was clear a real civil war was about to happen. He didn't need to know the winner because whoever took over his father's operation would be just as monstrous as he was.

Everyone had to die here.

Aden didn't care anymore about his brother and sisters that were just as bad and vulnerable and groomed as he was. They were all bad people and they all had to die so they couldn't hurt another soul.

"See Isabella," Aden said, "this is what you've caused. You killed the only man that could ever unite everyone under his banner. The Crimson Gauntlet was a Crime Family of power, riches and influence and you have just killed that,"

"Of course," Isabella said. "That's the point because I have always lied about my plan,"

Aden laughed. Isabella was always full of

surprises as she revealed Blackout was on her wrist and the watch-like device was humming, vibrating and fizzing a little.

"You've connected to the main systems," Marcus said. "That's impossible,"

"Nothing is impossible dear boy if you simply forget about the rules of man,"

Aden noticed there was something in the distance. It looked like naval ships or something and that meant they were running out of time to escape.

"Ah yes," Isabella said. "Some stupid Naval ships are coming. Let me give you a small demonstration of my power,"

Isabella clicked Blackout and Aden didn't feel anything but he simply focused on the five Royal Navy ships coming towards them.

He noticed the ships start to slow before it looked like one was trying to turn but the water caught it at the wrong angle and it hit another ship then another then another.

Two ships flipped over and the other three sunk as they smashed into each other.

"All those lives now dead," Aden said. "You are exactly our Father's daughter,"

Bullets screamed through the air.

All the crew that were pointing their weapons at Isabella were dead. Their corpses landed with a thud.

"There is no support for the likes of you anymore," Isabella said as she clicked Blackout a final time. "That's it,"

Aden went forward but a man gripped his arm. "What's it?"

"The Final Command has been issued. Unless you can deactivate it or your MI5 friends can stop Blackout. The full power of Blackout will be unleashed in ten minutes. It will knock out all power in Europe and the UK,"

"Allowing Russia and China to storm through the continent within days," Marcus said.

"Exactly," Isabella said.

Aden shook the man's grip free as he watched Isabella go over to the massive windows as she smiled at the sea around her.

"There is no chance of you saving the day. Not this time," Isabella.

"Let's see about that," Aden said stomping on a guard's foot.

He screamed.

Aden grabbed his gun. Shooting him in the head.

Marcus charged forward.

Aden fired at the windows.

The windows shattered.

Marcus tackled Isabella.

They both fell out the window together.

CHAPTER 19
8th May 2023

Somewhere Off The Coast of France

Marcus hissed as he leapt with Isabella out the window of the bridge and they zoomed towards the immense ground below them.

The grey metal floor zoomed into view and Marcus just focused on making sure Isabella landed first.

She kicked him midair.

Marcus fell away from her.

He saw the ground getting close with shipping containers coming up.

Marcus shot out his hands.

He gripped the edge of one. The sheer force jerked him making him let go.

He fell to the ground.

When he landed with a thud Marcus hissed in pain as it pulsed up his legs and the rest of his entire body. He was surprised he was actually alive but that meant Isabella was alive too.

Static filled his ears and Marcus just knew his damn earpiece was broken now and he was completely alone with Isabella stalking the shipping containers.

Marcus went to take out his gun but realised he didn't have one. Those dumb crew members had taken his one earlier.

Isabella's laughter echoed all around him. It got louder and louder.

Marcus ducked.

A fist shot past him.

Marcus spun around.

Isabella punched him in the jaw.

He slammed into a shipping container.

She kicked him.

Again. Again.

Ramming his head into the shipping container.

Marcus collapsed to the ground.

Marcus grabbed her foot.

Pulling it to one side.

She fell.

Marcus jumped on top of her.

She slashed him with his nails.

Cutting into his skin.

Marcus screamed in pain.

She headbutted him.

Punched him.

Kicked him.

Marcus fell to one side.

Isabella got up and pressed one of her boots into his throat making Marcus gag a little.

"I had so much hope for you. I thought you were going to be a good fighter and a worthy kill," Isabella said.

Marcus grabbed her boot and she was surprised by the sheer strength. He lifted the boot off her throat.

She tried to put all her weight on it. Marcus didn't care. He lifted it off his throat.

Marcus threw her to one side.

Marcus leapt up. He flew at her.

Marcus kicked her.

Gripped the back of her head.

He ripped out her hair.

He spun her around.

Aiming her at the shipping container.

She jumped up.

Kicking herself off the shipping container.

Marcus fell backwards.

He hit something.

His vision blurred.

He saw a gun.

He leapt forward.

He smashed into Isabella.

He felt the gun.

Marcus pushed it away from him.

She fired it.

Shots screamed off into the air.

Marcus elbowed her in the ribs.

Isabella kicked him in-between the legs.

Marcus dropped like a stone and as his vision cleared all he could see was Isabella's smiling face that was laughing at him.

Marcus hated the woman. He had no idea how such a stupid woman could be so cold, awful and foul towards other people. He almost pitied her but he had seen what she did to people she didn't like.

She deserved everything she ever got in life.

Isabella pointed her gun at his head. "I'll give you a quick death but I will so enjoy killing my little brother. I will make his death slow and painful so that by the end he is begging for death,"

Marcus just frowned at her. How dare the bitch want to kill that hot sexy man that had given up everything to save him. Sure Aden might have betrayed him. But Aden also freed him, tried to save the world and he had even shot out the window to help him.

That meant something to Marcus and it didn't matter if Aden wasn't typical boyfriend material. In this line of work it didn't matter because Marcus did love Aden.

So he would protect him to the end and that all started with killing this bitch.

Marcus leapt up so quickly the world blurred.

He charged at Isabella.

He gripped her wrists.

His fingernails digging into her flesh.

She screamed in pain.

Marcus whacked the gun from her grip.

He grabbed her head.

Ramming it into the shipping container.

Her head landed with a thud.

She screamed out in pain.

Marcus didn't stop.

He kept whacking her head again and again.

Something cracked. Isabella screamed in agony.

He kept going.

Marcus kept smashing until there was nothing left to smash into the shipping container and his hands were covered in blood and Isabella's corpse landed with a thud.

He knelt down next to the body and carefully took Blackout off her wrist and he felt his stomach twist into a painful knot.

He wasn't a computer expert. He didn't know how to save the world, he didn't know how to deactivate Blackout.

Marcus did the only logical thing he could do in the situation. He placed the watch-like device on the ground and he stomped on it.

Again and again until Blackout was all gone and there was nothing left for anything to use or rebuild.

Marcus couldn't deny he felt a little dead inside considering that he had failed in his mission in more ways than he cared to remember. He hadn't retrieved Blackout and maybe he was a failure in the eyes of MI5 but he just sort of knew he had helped to make the world and the UK a safer place today.

All because no one could ever use Blackout again and at least the world wasn't in danger from a stupid UK defence programme that Marcus seriously didn't believe should have happened in the first place.

Now Marcus just had one more thing to do. He had to talk with the beautiful man he loved and just see if there was a future for them together and he really wanted to prove to himself that love doesn't betray everyone in the end.

CHAPTER 20
8th May 2023
Somewhere off The Coast Of France

As Aden got the last of his knives out of the corpses scattered around the bridge he couldn't believe how his life had changed now and he really didn't know what was going to happen in the future for him. The future was a complete mystery but he supposed it could have been as light or dark as he liked depending on what he wanted for it.

Aden laughed to himself as he leant against the icy coldness of the wall of the bridge. He had never had the chance to think about what he wanted for his future before, he had never wanted to be homeless or abandoned and once his father had found him he had never been given a choice. He had always just done what he was told so he could be "loved", survive and not end up on the streets again.

It really was that simple.

Aden wasn't a massive fan of the strange taste

that formed on his tongue from the salty sea air as it mixed with the iron tang of the vapourised blood in the air. He didn't doubt there would be attacks against them all day because of the odd crew members that had survived but Aden didn't mind.

He didn't want to kill them and he would always give them a choice of getting arrested or dying in a pointless fight. He knew most of them would choose the latter but he still liked himself for wanting to give them a choice.

It was even something his father would have been proud of.

"Hello beautiful," Marcus said as he came in and he placed his gun on the wooden table that was a lot more bloody and covered in corpses than when he had left.

Aden put his knives away and he supposed this was the best time they were going to talk about their future. A future he wanted a lot more than he wanted to admit.

"You look good even without your suit on," Marcus said.

Aden laughed. He couldn't believe how calm, wonderful and breathtaking Marcus was even though they had been through betrayal, attempted murders and international crimes together. Marcus was still the hot, sexy and stunning man that Aden had met two days ago.

"Do you really want to do this? We only met two days ago?" Aden asked.

"I do," Marcus said slowly coming over to him. "Because I've been an intelligence officer for five years now and I know meeting hot, incredible men is seriously hard and I don't want to spend another day alone,"

Aden wasn't sure that was the most romantic thing he had ever heard but he was interested in hearing more.

"Aden, you're a beautiful man and I love you more than anything," Marcus said knowing he wanted to hear more. "I know we have both had our struggles but I believe in you more than you will ever know,"

Aden took a few steps closer to him and placed a loving hand on his arm. He really liked how smooth and warm his arms were against his fingers.

"What's going to happen to me?"

Marcus hugged him gently at first but as Aden wrapped his arms around Marcus's fit body he tightened his arms. So much so that Aden enjoyed the warm feeling of Marcus's breath on his neck.

"I honestly don't know but nothing bad will happen because you helped me. You fixed this and you helped to save everyone. If you tell us everything about your father then I'm sure you won't serve any prison time,"

Aden smiled at that. Marcus, always the hot stunning man that focused on law and order and everything that good citizens did. Aden really did love that about him.

Aden kissed him softly. They might have only met two days ago but Aden really loved the soft, warmth of his lips against his. Marcus was definitely the best kisser he had ever had the pleasure of meeting and he really liked having him in his life.

And he just sort of knew without a shadow of a doubt that whatever happened now until and beyond the time that they were rescued by the French Coastguard that everything would be okay. Aden had Marcus by his side, he had a man who loved him and Aden really, really couldn't believe how lucky he was to have found them.

Life was great and Aden was so looking forward to spending the rest of his life with such a stunning man. And maybe they would even get to travel the UK together protecting the country and fighting side by side.

Now that would be a hell of a lot of fun.

CHAPTER 21
3rd June 2023
London, England

If anyone had asked Marcus if the next month would have been so fun, enjoyable and simply the best month of his life then he would have called them a liar but they would have turned out to be completely correct.

Marcus still couldn't believe how much fun he had had travelling round the UK with beautiful, sexy Aden by his side as they fought to destroy and clean up the rest of Harald's organisation now that it was in complete chaos. They had travelled together killing, loving and laughing along the way from the top of Scotland all the way down to the very southern tip of England.

Marcus hugged the wonderful man he was loving more and more with each passing day as they both sat on a double-seated camping chair as they watched Ryan coach his little football team. There was a big match tomorrow and Marcus knew they were going to absolutely smash it all because Ryan was an amazing coach, brother and person.

Marcus was really impressed with the great weather for a change as the bright intense sun shone down bathing everything in a rich golden light. He was glad the white lines of the huge football pitch had faded just a little otherwise he might have been blinded.

The car park behind him was full of young happy families out with their children and Marcus enjoyed hearing them laughing, screaming with happiness and playing in the distance in the nearby playground.

They were all safe, happy and Marcus loved his job because of it. It was even better they would never ever know what almost happened to them because of Blackout.

Something MI5 might admitted never happened in the first place so Marcus could never be rewarded or punished for destroying the multi-billion-pound project.

Marcus wrapped his arms around wonderful Aden as he whistled and cheered as one of the kids scored his first-ever goal and that was great fun. Marcus hadn't realised that Aden had such a knack for helping children but Marcus supposed he really shouldn't have been surprised.

As the past month had told him over and over, Aden was a very special, resourceful and loving man that really did just want to help everyone who needed it. He had helped a lot of homeless children up in Manchester, he had helped elderly ladies in London and he had helped food banks in Cornwall.

Marcus still understood it himself but maybe that was because he had always had people that loved him surrounding him. Ryan and his sister were great, Aria and Jessica were his work family and now Aden was his boyfriend.

Something that Ryan was extremely pleased about and Marcus was looking forward to actually spending time with his brother more and his own family. Ryan and his family had taken to Aden instantly and Marcus was now almost worried that he wasn't the family favourite anymore.

Not that it mattered much.

Because him and Aden were a couple that loved each other so much that they could handle anything the world could throw at them. It didn't matter if a terrorist attacked, a bomb went off, even missiles couldn't stop them because they had each other. And that seriously did mean something to Marcus.

And he loved Aden for it.

A delightfully warm breeze blew across the football pitch and Marcus grinned as more and more kids kicked the ball into the goal so artfully that he suspected Aden had been secretly teaching them something without him knowing. The kids seemed so happy, Marcus was more than happy with his life and he was so glad that he was sitting next to the man he loved.

Marcus looked behind him as Aria and Jessica got out of the car and they both smiled at him and Marcus just laughed. One day he was finally going to be able to simply enjoy his Saturdays with his brother, the team and Aden but that wasn't today.

And as Marcus said goodbye to the kids and his brother and simply took Aden by the hand off towards their next mission, Marcus couldn't deny his life was amazing and he wouldn't change anything for the entire world. Because Marcus definitely couldn't get better than this.

DAMAGE, HEALING, LOVE

CONNOR WHITELEY

No part of this book may be reproduced in any form or by any electronic or mechanical means. Including information storage, and retrieval systems, without written permission from the author except for the use of brief quotations in a book review.

This book is NOT legal, professional, medical, financial or any type of official advice

Any questions about the book, rights licensing, or to contact the author, please email connorwhiteley@connorwhiteley.net

Copyright © 2024 CONNOR WHITELEY

All rights reserved.

CHAPTER 1
23rd January 2024
Canterbury, England

"Why are we going to this Fair thing?"

Zach James just laughed and pulled his best friend, Lora, in the entire world in for a massive hug as they went up a long terribly tarmacked path with thick oak, pine and beech trees lining it. He shivered a little as he watched his breathe condense and formed thick columns of vapour.

He sort of felt like a dragon. He breathed heavily and just smiled as the thick columns shot out his nose. The air was great with hints of grass, damp and freshly cut wood that only helped to make the day even better.

Zach had always really liked the smell of cut wood. It reminded him of being home with his Mum, Dad and two brothers who helped their Dad on their tree farm. Zach had never actually cared too much about the farm but it was sustainably done so he supposed he shouldn't have minded that much.

The sky above was grey but at least it wasn't going to rain and it wasn't wet. Zach really didn't like going out when it was wet and cold, it was so draining and there was nothing better than being in-doors with friends and a boyfriend.

Not that Zach actually had a boyfriend even more because of… an old friend called Jayden. Zach shook the thought away because thinking about Jayden, what they had done to each other and how innocent Jayden was, was never a good idea.

"Why?" Lora asked like a small child.

Zach shook his head and just smiled at his best friend. She always did look great with her long blond hair that ran down to the top of her legs, her green jacket showed off her thin body and she was really fun to be around.

She was brilliant, but she clearly didn't see the benefit of going to the Big Fair.

"Because I want to look at the Societies, which before you ask because I know you're a big kid at heart. They are what the university calls adult social clubs and no I do not know, why they are called Societies," Zach said.

They both smiled and Zach focused back on the tarmacked path. It was rather nice not seeing any other students on it, normally when he went to his lectures the path was packed full of students and it was a free for all.

It was even worse when it was raining or had just

rained. And the wide stretches of grass to the side of the path turned into mud baths and sadly the trees provided little to no cover.

The sound of birds, cars and students in the far distance made Zach realise they were coming up to the university campus. The last time he had been up this path was before Winter Break so he hadn't realised how far and close everything was at different points.

"Why do you want us to do a society together?" Lora asked. "We already spent so much time together, so why don't you admit the real reason you want me to come along?"

Zach forced himself not to stop in his tracks, so he kept on walking. He didn't want to tell Lora how he had been spending so much time with her and still wanted to be with her constantly just so he didn't have to think about Ryan. Ryan had left him, shattered his heart and just wrecked him because of what Jayden had innocently done.

Zach shook his head. He couldn't start thinking about Jayden and what had happened last August. It wasn't healthy. It wasn't good and he would only start getting depressed again.

He couldn't go back to that place, so he lied.

"The real reason is because we have both been living in my flat and talking with my flatmates for the past four months. We need to get out and see people," Zach said.

"Sure, sure," Lora said smiling.

"It's the truth and I know we both have other friends, and once a week we go out to Q-Bar with six people. But I want to actually *do* something more,"

Lora laughed. "Darling, you haven't *done* anyone for two months,"

Zach flinched a little and tried to grin and smile. It didn't really work and he was going to have to tell Lora that he didn't want reminders of Ryan. It was true him and Ryan had been very active in the bedroom and Ryan had left him in November after struggling for months.

He just didn't need to be reminders of it.

"I am sorry you know. I really am and I won't mention it again," Lora said knowing he didn't like reminders of Ryan. "How about we look at a baking society? We both like baking, right?"

Zach laughed as they went towards a little black path that shot away from the one they were currently on. It was a shortcut towards the Sports Hall where the Big Fair was happening.

Zach had no idea if he actually liked Baking or not because he had never tried it. But if it meant meeting new people, making new friends and getting out back into the world then he was certainly up for it.

And that excited him a lot more than he ever wanted to admit.

CHAPTER 2
23rd January 2024
Canterbury, England

University student Jayden Baker was so excited as he laid on his back on his soft, warm, cosy single bed in his university flat. He couldn't wait for his friends to knock on his door so they could go to The Big Fair together at the university. An event that Jayden really hoped would allow him to join new social groups, new activities and meet new people.

Maybe even a boyfriend.

Jayden sat up a little on his bed and hissed a little as the icy coldness of the flat's white walls chilled him a lot more than he wanted to admit. He had only gotten back to Kent University last week but he was still getting used to the cold winters. And how the university's apartment buildings failed to keep out much of the cold.

Jayden really liked the flat though. It might have been a bit pricey (which was why his parents were thankfully paying for it), but it was great and it was home. He was so glad the university had allowed him to put up some of his favourite landscape photos that he had taken. He had loved the trips from the hilly landscapes of Wales and the rough coastline of Cornwall and the stunning sunsets he had gotten in the Lake District.

He flat out loved photography and managing to actually capture a moment like the viewer was really there. That was the whole point of taking a photo.

Jayden heard a hiss as his automatic air fresher (a little Christmas gift from his mother) was activated. He still needed to find out how to turn the silly thing off but he liked the calming notes of fig and amber and there were some hints there that he wasn't too sure about. They were probably violet and jasmine but he wasn't sure, but they did smell great.

He could almost taste the great fig pie his grandmother used to make. Jayden had always loved that as a kid with whipped cream, strawberries and the most intense vanilla ice cream he had ever tasted.

A buzzing sound filled the flat.

Jayden leant across the tiny gap that was between his bed and his wooden "desk". That was actually nothing more than a very nice sheet of walnut wood that stretched the entire length of the flat (all five metres of it) with a desk chair. Not a traditional desk but Jayden didn't mind.

Jayden picked up his phone and took out the charger. He grinned as his best friends in the entire world Caroline, Kate and Jackie were coming to his flat now. Jayden was glad he was going to see them because he hadn't seen them since they went up North for the winter break.

Jayden wasn't exactly sure why he wanted to go to the Big Fair. It was a massive event where all the social group or Societies as they preferred to be called, got to advertise themselves again and students could see them.

He had gone to Freshers' fair back in September, but Jayden tensed a little because that really wasn't the best time to look for new, stressful and scary events.

Jayden hated how he had just recovered from his breakdown, how he had just lost all his friends and how he had needed to see a therapist intensely for a month. She was brilliant and Jayden couldn't thank her enough for all the amazing things she had said and done for him.

But he hadn't wanted to do many societies. He had been happy enough when he met Caroline, Kate and Jackie at an Art Social for all the Art students at the university. That had been bad enough.

Jayden hissed as his heart rate increased. His ears rang and he simply forced himself to count out of order. He was still surprised it worked, but apparently the brain couldn't focus on panicking and counting at the same time.

Three women laughed outside and Jayden just grinned as he leapt off his bed and opened it for them.

Jayden was so happy to see Caroline in her thick winter coat (she was always cold even in the height of summer) and Kate in her blue shorts and summer shirt (she was always too hot). And Jayden just hugged Jackie and really liked her sweet coconut perfume.

He felt a little underdressed compared to his friends. He was only wearing blue jeans, black trainers and a black hoody that wasn't even a designer one. Compared to the women that all looked great, wonderful and almost seductive.

"Come on Jayden," Caroline said. "Let's go and see the Societies. There might be that baking one or LGBT+ society you wanted to visit,"

"Watch out Caroline," Kate said grinning. "It might be too cold for you,"

Caroline stuck her tongue out. "No, watch out yourself Kate. It might be too hot for you with all those university students. That's a lot of body heat,"

Jayden smiled. He really had missed his friends.

Jackie hugged Jayden again. "Let's just see if Baking society is on,"

Jayden pretended to roll his eyes out of boredom. There was nothing he would like more than to go to Baking society because he loved cooking. It was so relaxing, fun and the best part was he could eat it.

Jayden was so excited as he left his flat and he was looking forward to putting his past behind him and making new friends. Friends that he wouldn't hurt and friends that wouldn't hurt him almost as badly.

At least he ever had to see anyone from that part of his life again.

Little did know Jayden realise the exact opposite was about to happen.

CHAPTER 3
23rd January 2024
Canterbury, England

Zach seriously supposed he should have realised the reason why the Big Fair was called the Big Fair, but it was absolutely massive. He had been in the Sports Hall before and he was always shocked the central hall alone was the size of a football pitch and then there were two other halls that were only slightly smaller than a football pitch on each side.

The Big Fair made use of all the different halls and even some of the small rooms where the University's sports teams met, had their training meetings and teaching stuff.

Zach stood to one side of the massive blue doors to the Sports Hall and he was amazed at the scale of it. He had his back pressed against the perfectly warm green block walls and to his left a river of students washed into the fair.

He had never seen so many students of all

shapes, sizes and ages come together. There were a lot of students in blue, black and even white jeans. A lot of them were designer ones along with the matching designer shirt but Zach didn't mind too much.

Some of the men were seriously hot.

Zach focused on one group of friends in particular as they came in. He couldn't help but focus on their sexy large asses in their black jeans as they stood near him and Lora and decided where to start. They were all wearing designer shirts that highlighted their fit bodies and long black curly hair.

They all looked identical but they were all hot.

"Someone's enjoying themselves," Lora said smiling. "You're grinning like a teenager,"

Zach tried to frown but those men were hot, and it was only now he was realising just how long it had been since he had been out and about and allowed himself to check out men.

He had really missed the feeling.

"What row do you want to start in?" Lora asked.

Zach rolled his eyes as he actually looked for the first time at where the river of students were flowing to. It was a nightmare and there were so many societies to cover.

He realised the Big Fair in the central hall was split out into three rows with different stalls lining each one. Zach couldn't see that much because of the sheer amount of students there but there were things on each stall including swag and other freebies. Zach loved freebies.

There were different things on often for each stall and some of them looked a lot more interesting than others. Like there was marketing society with two large women standing behind it offering people free mugs, but the stall next to it was only offering pens.

Zach still wanted to see both.

"Come on," Lora said.

Zach allowed her to drag him into the massive group of students and they slowly shuffled towards the first row of stalls. He could barely see what the stalls were because there were so many students with the smells of sweat, perfume and manly musk filling the hall. Zach seriously didn't mind the scent of manly musk.

He wanted to roll his eyes because he was only realising now how long it had truly been since he had allowed himself to focus on men. And men were beautiful people.

Zach gently guided Lora forward through a small gap between two different friendship groups, who in their divine wisdom, had just decided to stand in the middle of the row making it hard for others to get round them.

He hated people like that.

Zach pushed Lora forward and they glided through a large group of students until he accidentally found himself at the University Football Society. Zach just grinned like a schoolboy at the rich aroma of manly musk and sweat as he looked at the blue and black football kit the three striking men were wearing behind the little bench.

Zach had no idea why the men felt the need to wear their "used" kit to get new members, but he was hardly complaining.

The man with the words "Team Captain" on the front of his football shirt smiled. "You're Zach, right?"

"Yeah," Zach said wanting to take a step back but he couldn't because of the wall of students behind him.

"I'm Colin. I'm Ryan's new boyfriend. I've heard a lot about you. Do you want to join?"

The words struck Zach like bullets and stab wounds and the entire world just fell away from him. He could see Colin's lips move and he didn't doubt other people were talking about him but he just couldn't hear a word.

This couldn't be happening. He had wanted to move on from Ryan and that part of his life. He couldn't be doing this. He didn't want to be reminded of Ryan and what he had lost.

Zach shook his head and pushed his way through the other students and when his hearing returned he simply kept on gliding through the crowd.

"Talk to me," Lora said.

Zach shook his head and he was glad when he spotted the Baking Society up ahead. He could just focus on that, he was safe and he could deal with

Colin and Ryan later on. Right now he could pretend he was fine and nothing bad was happening.

"Excuse me please," Zach said as he made his way through the crowd with Lora close behind him.

After a few moments of passing art students in long red, colourful dresses, he found himself right next to the Baking stall and he was so happy it was filled with little samples of cookies.

Exactly what he needed after that awful encounter.

"So how much is it for the rest of the year?" Jayden asked.

Zach looked to see who was standing right next to him and as much as he wanted to frown or panic, he couldn't believe he was standing right next to the most striking, stunning man he had ever met.

But also the man that had damaged, hurt and wrecked him because of an innocent mistake.

CHAPTER 4
23rd January 2024
Canterbury, England

Jayden flat out couldn't believe how packed the Big Fair was as he went into the Sports Hall. He had never been interested in Sports, he actually hated them but the hall was massive. He supposed it could have been the size of a football pitch but he had no idea what the size of them were. It was an expression that he fully intended to use.

He followed Jackie, Caroline and Katie around through the sea of students up and down the long rows of little stalls. He had wanted to make a little more progress than they currently were but there were simply too many students in all their different clothes, ages and heights walking about.

Jayden rolled his eyes as Caroline pulled them all towards a little wooden table where the Knitting Society (of all things) had set up shop. He had never ever seen the point in knitting, because it was something that old ladies did and Caroline was not an old lady.

But the stall looked nice enough. There were all sorts of red, purple and blue balls of wool on the wooden table. Jayden didn't like the look of the long grey knitting needles but he supposed he could have positioned them in a way that would make the moment come alive.

The vivid colours of the wool mixed with the Sports Hall lighting (which wasn't actually that bad) and the monotone knitting needles were all things he could work with. Jayden nodded to himself because he would have really liked to do that.

The rich, fruity, citrus smells of oranges, lime and lemons filled the stall as a group of young women in tank tops, skirts and little tiny handbags came over. Jayden wanted to cough but he forced himself not too, he didn't want to be rude.

But that aroma was way too strong for his liking.

"And if I knit something how warm would that keep me?" Caroline asked. "The problem is I am always cold,"

Jayden just laughed, because he really did love Caroline as a friend. She was hopeless, always concerned about keeping warm and she was just funny.

Jayden looked at some of the other stalls but it was hard with the wall of other students in his way. He could see a football Society on the other side and Jayden shook his head.

He couldn't imagine him playing football or any sport to be honest. He loved masculine and sporty men but he wasn't into it himself. It was just so damn pointless grown men running around after a ball for 90 minutes. What was the point? They were going to get tired and sweaty and it just didn't achieve anything. Sure it might have been entertaining for some people but to Jayden it was just so, so pointless.

"Oh Jayden," Kate said. "There's baking society over there. Come on,"

"But I haven't finished with knitting Society," Caroline said.

Jayden shrugged. "Join us when you're done, because I have a feeling Katie's getting hot just looking and thinking about wool,"

"Awh you do get me," Katie said giving Jayden a mocking hug and a kiss on the cheek.

Jayden gently took his best friend's hand and they fought through the immense crowd of students. This crowd all mainly seemed to be made up of hot fit sporty men in tight jeans, shirts and their aftershave was so overwhelming with hints of aromantic apple and rose that Jayden was rather turned-on.

Jayden made his way over to the Baking Society stall that was a lot busier than he expected. He stood to one side as the two smiling, clearly happy women in their blue t-shirts were talking to a bunch of other students.

The stall itself was great and Jayden so badly

wanted to help himself to the different samples of chocolate, vanilla and maybe chilli cookies that were on the wooden table. There were pictures of the society's events, their social media details and Jayden had to admit this all looked great.

He couldn't help but smile to himself because he felt like him joining baking society might be a good idea. It would be fun, he would get to meet people and he would get to do tons of fun stuff in the long-term.

The other students moved away and Jayden went with Katie over to the two women who looked really happy to see them. Jayden noticed there was someone else standing next to him, a blond man, but Jayden didn't pay him any attention even though the smell was very familiar.

And very nice.

"So how much is the society for the rest of the year?" Jayden asked.

Out of the corner of his eye he noticed the blond man had turned to look at him and Jayden turned to see who the hell this blond man was.

Fucking hell. He was stunning and he was the man that Jayden had hurt so, so badly.

Jayden's heart pounded in his chest. His chest felt like it was going to explode. His ears rang.

Cold sweat ran down his back. His mouth turned dry. His stomach filled with butterflies and churned and then it felt like an angry cat was inside his stomach.

And then he realise Zach really was beautiful and so damn attractive and striking. He looked as great now as he had back in July and August.

Jayden really loved how Zach was still so insanely fit, sexy and his black t-shirt highlighted how Zach didn't have any body fat, he was so lean and toned without having any muscles. His face was still so perfect and lovely to look at, with his slightly pointy chin, his light blue eyes and his smooth perfect skin. Yet Jayden was so glad Zach was still a hot, seductive blond with his hair parted to the right so it covered his forehead and Zach just looked so strikingly masculine and perfect.

Zach moved a little on the spot and Jayden realised that was the smell he had missed. There was always the subtle smell of manly musk about Zach that had always turned on and made him horny around Zach, but he had fallen in love (toxic love but love nonetheless) in August not because of Zach's perfectly seductive twink body, but because he was one of the nicest people Jayden had ever met.

Now he just needed to know if Zach was still angry at him for all the damage he had caused.

GAY ROMANCE COLLECTION VOLUME 4

CHAPTER 5
23rd January 2024
Canterbury, England

As much as Zach wanted to say, believe and shout that it was bad seeing Jayden again, he just couldn't. He didn't really know what it was but as his heart rate calmed down and some of the dryness of his mouth went away, he realised that Jayden was still a really good-looking guy.

He might not have had much brown hair but his cute face was all lines and angles and Zach had always liked Jayden's deep hazelnut eyes. They were so alert, so full of life and Jayden had always looked at him in a really caring way. Zach had always liked that about him because they both cared so much about each other last August.

Zach couldn't help but smile as he subtly checked out Jayden's rather fit body again. Zach didn't mind that he had some meat on his bones as his mother used to say but Jayden was still fit, cute and he looked so good.

It was only then that Zach realised he had sort of

wanted this chance to meet again. Sure they had seen each other around campus, they had walked past each other and Jayden had tried to say hello. But Zach always stayed silent and kept on walking because he wasn't sure what he would say.

He certainly didn't know what he was meant to say now. He didn't know what Jayden was like, if he had changed or anything. Zach didn't want to talk to Jayden if he was still the same intense, obsessive and overwhelming person he had been in August.

Zach shook at the idea. He couldn't go back but he wanted to see if Jayden was okay, and it wouldn't be a bad thing to see if this cute man was okay.

"How are you?" Jayden asked.

Zach forced himself to take a deep breath and he got an interesting hint of some kind of aromantic apple and rose aftershave.

"Let's go," Lora said pulling at Zach's arm a little.

Zach pulled away from her touch because he was a grown man and he did want to talk to cute Jayden.

"How are you?" Zach asked knowing full well he was dodging the question.

"Yeah I'm good thanks, a lot has changed since August. Therapy went really well, I've met a lot of new friends and life is great. I came out to my parents and my wider family and everyone has been so nice at home,"

Zach just grinned and forced himself not to hug Jayden. That was amazing news that he had come out to his family, it was all Zach had ever wanted for him because Jayden was such a nice guy and his family had taken such a toll on his mental health that it was brilliant to know Jayden had changed.

Zach frowned a little. He was surprised more than anything else because the last time he had seen Jayden, the idea of coming out to his family had been awful, like a death sentence so it must had taken a hell of lot of courage to do that.

"That's brilliant. I am so please for you," Zach said. "I hope things continue to go well and yeah,"

Jayden looked like he was about to reply when a large group of students slightly knocked into him. Zach went to moan at them but he forced himself not to. Jayden wasn't his friend anymore and Jayden could look after himself.

"Thanks, that really does mean a lot coming from you. I know it was something that you always wanted for me, so I'm really glad I did it. How about you? How's Ryan?"

Zach frowned. Jayden didn't know, he didn't know anything because that was how Zach had done their last messages and the ending of their relationship. He had blocked and partly ghosted Jayden on Instagram because it was better for everyone that way.

Zach couldn't believe Jayden didn't know the pain, the trouble and the consequences he had caused Ryan when he had messaged him to find out more about dealing with bad family members. Zach knew it was all his fault because he had told Jayden about Ryan's family when they started to be friends back in July, he hadn't realised Jayden would actually ask Ryan about it. Not that Zach told him it was an off-limit subject.

Zach had seriously screwed up.

"Me and Ryan broke up," Zach said forcing the fakest smile he had ever done. "It was for the best and yeah, Ryan has a new boyfriend after only two months,"

"Who's this?" a woman asked in a t-shirt and shorts.

Zach was a little annoyed that someone would interrupt him and Jayden, but over the sheer deafening noise of the other students he supposed that was bound to happen at some point.

"This is Zach," Jayden said, "and Zach, this is my new friend Katie,"

"Oh *that* Zach,"

Zach felt really cold all of a sudden and he had no idea what he wanted to do, he wanted to run, hide and just scream a little.

"What do you mean *that* Zach?" Zach asked wanting to know.

"Um, just that you hurt him and you wrecked Jayden," Katie said.

"No," Jayden said the panic clear in his voice. "Honestly I only told them at I hurt you badly and what happened between us is why I struggle with friendships,"

Zach shook his head. "I have to go. I have a thing. It was good seeing you and I'm glad you're okay,"

Before cute Jayden could say another word Zach went away and glided through all the different students again with Lora close behind him. He was annoyed with himself because as much as he didn't know how to handle the idea that Jayden had told others about what had happened, he only wanted to spend more and more time with Jayden.

He was so cute, so pretty and so fit but Zach just felt like there was more to it than that. He just had no idea why.

No idea at all.

CHAPTER 6
23rd January 2024
Canterbury, England

"I'm sorry Jayden,"

Jayden just waved Katie silent as they all sat around the little white chipboard table in Katie's university kitchen. He certainly didn't like Katie's cheaper accommodation compared to his own because the kitchen was rather awful. It was so small and clinical with its dirty white walls, white cabinets and white kitchen table that was so clearly made of chipboard that it just looked so cheap.

Jayden didn't like to be a snob but it was the truth. There was nothing luxurious or even that nice about the kitchen and it was even worse that some of Katie's flatmates had left a small takeaway container filled with mash potatoes, a steak and gravy. Yet judging by the cracked surface of the gravy, it had been uncovered for ages and that was just disgusting.

The only thing Jayden did like about the kitchen

was the fact that Katie, Caroline and Jackie were with him. They all had their bags of freebies and swag arranged on the table, and some of it looked really cool.

Jayden was so impressed that Caroline had gotten a whole bunch of free knitwear including a blue scarf, two red jumpers and some green gloves. She was wearing the scarf now and like always she complained that she was too cold.

Maybe Jackie had gotten the most useful freebies and swag at the Big Fair, because Jayden really liked the three mugs she had "borrowed" from different stalls, and the pens, notepads and other free things were impressive.

Katie had managed to grab some freebies but there was barely anything. And Jayden didn't have anything.

After what had happened with Zach and Katie's wonderful little bombshell, Jayden had sort of walked around the Big Fair like a zombie. He felt so numb, so cold and so emotionless that he didn't know what to feel.

Katie passed Jayden a piping hot mug of coffee, and Jayden really liked the bitter, rich aromas that hit his nose.

"You've told us the story in various ways," Jackie said, "but what actually happened between you, Zach and Ryan?"

Jayden laughed. "God that really is a story and a half but I think I need to tell you,"

"Definitely," all three women said leaning closer like this was the start of a child's story time.

"So I first met Zach about a year ago, he was fucking beautiful and he stood out to me immediately. He was cute, funny and he was just amazing with his blond hair. And we spoke a little but we didn't really do anything else because we didn't really talk, talk,"

"Okay that sounds fine so far," Katie said fanning herself like she was still too hot.

Jayden nodded. "Then back in May we got talking a lot more, we exchanged information on Instagram and then May to July we spoke a fair bit. We made each other laugh, smile and we spoke about Ryan, his boyfriend. It was the start of a good friendship,"

"Okay," Jackie said a little tense.

"Then in July, Zach messaged me saying how he wanted to meet up so we went out. And over the course of the next four weeks we developed a very fast, very caring and very intense friendship. Like we loved spending time together, but I developed a problem,"

"You fell in love?" Caroline asked wrapping her arms around herself because she was still cold. "And you mentioned before you developed Emotional Dependency on him?"

"Exactly," Jayden said, "because my family was so bad towards me being gay and Jayden accepted me without question, I sort of *needed* him to feel loved, safe and secure in myself so that made our friendship very toxic in the end. But he always wanted to support me no matter what happened and no matter how intense I got,"

"He did care about you," Katie said.

"Absolutely," Jayden said. "Like Zach is one of the most caring people I have ever met and he is amazing. And honestly… I did love him truly because he was everything I wanted in a man,"

Jayden didn't like it how his friends didn't look convinced and he couldn't blame them at all. He knew how it sounded, he knew it sounded like he didn't love Zach he was only using Zach for his validation and had a minor obsession with Zach.

An obsession he did not have any more.

"So you had an intense and toxic friendship," Caroline said, "so what broke it?"

Jayden laughed nervously and he just focused on his coffee mug.

"Oh this is going to be good," Caroline said.

"Well," Jayden said, "the problem was I met Ryan. I had been wanting to meet Ryan for ages because I knew Zach really loved him and I honestly wanted to see a gay relationship. But seeing Zach so happy, so in love and so great with someone else, that in itself didn't bother me. But what scared me was the fact that I didn't believe I could ever have that happiness,"

"Why not?" Jackie asked.

"Because of my past and my family. I just didn't think I could have that level of happiness so I just sort of spiralled from there. I was so scared of losing Zach that I tried to become friends with Ryan, but I was way too intense. And I asked him about his own family, the family they don't talk too anymore,"

"And you upset him," Caroline said rubbing her hands together to keep warm.

"Yeah because then Zach messaged me that he didn't want to be friends anymore. Zach was wrong to have shared something so personal and delicate about Ryan's life without his permission and I was being too intense,"

"And that's what led to your breakdown," Katie said not asking but knowing.

Jayden nodded and he took a large sip of the wonderfully bitter and rich coffee.

"How are you feeling now after seeing and talking to Zach again?" Katie asked.

Jayden was about to answer when his phone buzzed and he realised he had a message on Instagram.

Zach had messaged him and that both scared and excited Jayden a lot more than he ever wanted to admit.

CHAPTER 7
23rd January 2024
Canterbury, England

Zach didn't exactly know why he had contacted Jayden but as he looked at his phone just waiting for that annoyingly cute man to reply, he couldn't help but feel so excited and also a little nervous. It was clear that Jayden had changed, he was healthier and he wasn't as intense or needy when they had spoken earlier, but Zach really didn't want to rush into anything.

Zach laid on Lora's bright pink bed, that looked rather horrible in a way, as him and Lora watched a comedy film she raved about. Zach didn't exactly see the appeal and given how much time he had spent in this flat over the past four months, he supposed he should have been used to it by now.

But he looked over to her little desk and there was a wide rack of shelves above it, and there was a row of three large teddies that somehow managed to look elegant and rather adult. Zach just didn't like the one in the middle with the dark eyes that felt like it was staring into his soul.

It was so off-putting.

Lora moved around on the bed and Zach looked up at her as she was laughing, smiling and really enjoying the comedy. She had pulled her long blond hair up into a pony tail and he so badly wanted to talk about today with her, but she had shared her feelings earlier.

She wasn't happy and she did nothing but berate, talk and just complain about Jayden. He understood why she had done it because she had seen how badly Jayden had hurt Ryan and him and their relationship, but the thing was Jayden was never a bad person. He was just really traumatised and he didn't know how things worked and he struggled a lot with friends. Especially gay ones.

It was why Zach had put up with Jayden for so long, but he always felt great, happy and light around Jayden because Jayden was a great guy. And he was so sweet and nice, but it was intense at times.

"Who are you texting?" Lora asked as she stopped the film as it ended.

Zach smiled because he really couldn't tell her that he was messaging Jayden. She wouldn't like that and he would never hear the end of it.

He had only sent Jayden, a message of *Hi, it was nice seeing you today. I'm glad your life's getting better.*

It wasn't too nice, leading or anything it was just

a matter of facts. A good healthy way to start a conversation.

Zach smiled as Jayden replied. *Yes, it was nice seeing you today and life is really good thanks. My friends are nice. What you up to?*

Zach took a deep breath of the creamy pumpkin-spiced latte aroma with a rich splash of vanilla and toffee filled Lora's flat. He almost panicked at the idea of maybe Jayden was being intense again, but he was being silly. It was normal to ask people what they're up to.

Zach texted back. *Nothing much. Just watching a comedy with Lora. What about you?*

He was surprised he actually didn't want Jayden to text back saying that he was with a boyfriend or something. And Zach just rolled his eyes as his stomach filled with butterflies, it was annoying as hell he was finding Jayden cute, fit and he couldn't stop thinking about Jayden's sweet eyes that were so full of life.

"Who are you texting?" Lora asked coming over.

Zach hid his phone so she couldn't look, and he just knew he was going to have to lie to her. Not because he wanted to but because he wanted to save himself from an evening of being told "don't you remember how much he hurt you and you're making a massive mistake,"

"I'm texting a guy," Zach said, "and it hurt like hell knowing that Ryan's moved on and dating someone like Colin, so I wanted to meet someone,"

Lora folded her arms. "And you just happened to have someone ready to talk to just like that,"

Zach nodded like he was a player and he had a million hot sexy men he could contact for some fun at the drop of a pin.

"Of course, I am very hot according to a lot of men," Zach said, "and why do you care so much?"

Lora went over to her desk and took a long sip of her latte. "Because I don't want you contacting Jayden. He hurt you and it was awful seeing you go through that,"

Zach nodded but he didn't like it. When him and Jayden had gone out a few times, Jayden had talked a lot about how his mother and family controlled who he could see and whatnot, apparently Jayden's parents thought the two of them were dating for those months.

An idea that made Zach smile, because Jayden was a cute, caring guy that just wanted the best for the people in his life. Zach supposed it wouldn't be a terrible idea to see about dating, but he had to know Jayden was different before he committed to anything.

He was not going back to the way things were in August. Lora was right, that was hell for him too.

"I'm not talking to Jayden because you're right. He really hurt me, he caused me and Ryan to break up by mistake and he just isn't the right guy for me," Zach said knowing he was lying because he actually wanted to meet up with Jayden so badly.

"Okay good," Lora said. "I'm going to the kitchen. Do you want anything?"

"No thanks," Zach said looking back at his phone.

I'm in my friend's kitchen talking about what happened today. I did like seeing you and I am sorry about Ryan. He was a great guy.

Zach couldn't help but smile. Jayden was always so sweet, so caring and such a great guy.

It's okay. Zach said not knowing if that was true or not. *I'm actually curious to see how much you're changed and um, what else you've been up to lately. Want to hang out sometime?*

As soon as Zach hit send he couldn't believe what the hell he had just done. He wanted this badly and it would be good if him and Jayden could be friends again and maybe even boyfriends, but he was nervous. Jayden was amazingly sweet but he could be so intense with his feelings. Zach didn't want to hurt him and he really didn't want Jayden to hurt him in return.

Sure I'm busy for the next few days with lectures and assignments but Saturday sounds good.

Zach was shocked and grinned like a schoolboy. The old Jayden would have said something like *any time is great* or Jayden would imply that he was prepared to drop everything he was doing or had planned to spend time with Zach.

But he wasn't like that anymore, Jayden was actually going to wait four days to see him.

And that was brilliant and Zach was so excited about Saturday. It could be brilliant or it could be awful.

CHAPTER 8
27ᵗʰ January 2024
Canterbury, England

Jayden flat out couldn't believe how brilliant, wonderful and lovely it had been just talking to Zach over the past few days. They hadn't spoken for very long or very deeply but it was nice just talking about university and whatnot. Jayden was glad that Zach was enjoying his course, he had made a bunch of friends that he sometimes hung out with and he was thinking about joining the Fencing Society.

Jayden seriously couldn't have cared less about Fencing or any sort of sports, but he couldn't deny the idea of Zach wearing sportswear was a massive turn-on. It would be good to see Zach's fit, sexy body without a gram of body fat covered in sportswear. Jayden just grinned to himself.

He was sitting on a rather cold wooden chair inside of one of the university's many little cafes and restaurants that were spread out all over campus.

Jayden rather liked this one because it was sort of an Italian joint with its warm cream colours, little photographs of Italy and the wonderful aromas of basil, tomatoes and garlic filled the café.

It was brilliant.

Jayden rested his arms on the slightly cold plastic table and really wanted Zach to hurry up so they could see each other. There were a lot of other students in the café because it was lunchtime and most of them were having a working lunch.

The table in front of Jayden was filled with a group of young women in hoodies, jeans and they all had their laptops out. Some of them had yellow legal pads and they were debating some kind of group project that at least two of the women hated with a passion. A rather cute waiter went over to them with a tray full of pizza and that managed to make the two women smile a lot more.

Jayden smiled weakly at the waiter as he went pass and he looked at his own half-empty cup of coffee. The Italians (even fake ones like this café) really did know how to do great coffee with just the right amounts of sugar, milk and bitterness that left a good aftertaste on the tongue.

"Hey," Zach said.

Jayden looked over and just grinned like a little schoolboy as the most beautiful man he had ever seen came over to him. Zach looked so striking in his black t-shirt that highlighted how fit he was, how he didn't have any muscles but he was so lean and fit and

Jayden just wanted to hug him. And Zach's thin legs looked good in his black jeans and he was so stunningly perfect.

"Hi," Jayden said as he watched Zach take a seat and they sort of looked at each other and smiled.

Jayden had really missed Zach's smile because he was so cute and attractive when he did smile.

"I have no idea where to start," Jayden said. "All I know is a lot has happened and I respect you enough to let you decide what you want,"

Jayden was a bit surprised that Zach looked a little shocked. He supposed it was fair considering part of emotional dependency and Jayden making their friendship toxic was he had made it very one-sided by mistake. So maybe Zach was surprised he wanted a more equal one.

"Oh okay," Zach said. "Well hey, I contacted you because I want to see what happened to you and how your life is now, because I did care about you a lot. And I think I might still care about you but I don't know,"

"Okay, let's see how today goes and *you* can decide if you want a friendship or not and we can go really slow," Jayden said.

He was actually rather impressed with himself, because he had played out this situation a thousand times over the past few months in his head. Like what would he say or do if Zach ever wanted to get back together as friends and hopefully more now that he wasn't with Ryan.

And in some of the situations in his head, Jayden was sadly intense and said his feelings too soon, but he hadn't today. Something he was so glad about.

"Katie seems nice, how did you meet?"

Jayden laughed because that was sort of connected to his breakdown, so that was going to be interesting for sure.

"So after you and me stopped being friends and after everything I did to get you back, I realised I needed more friends,"

"More friends besides me," Zach said smiling.

Jayden was glad Zach felt comfortable enough to make a small dig in his wonderfully caring voice that Jayden had missed.

"Yeah, because my breakdown was about gay stuff and my abuse and trauma. I found a little social club for gay young adults, like you said I should find, and that's how I met Katie. She's bi,"

"That's great and I'm glad you did take onboard what I said. That's why I told you and gave you those resources,"

Jayden really liked just talking, reconnecting and spending some time with such an attractive, fit and stunning man. And Jayden was surprised he wasn't anxious, scared and his ears weren't ringing like he had always expected them to if he had seen Zach again.

"Want to order some food?" Zach asked.

Jayden had been waiting for him to ask that because he wanted today to last as long as possible but he couldn't say it. Because the key to building a friendship first and maybe a relationship was to go slowly and that was exactly what Jayden intended to do.

Little did Jayden realise just how large the difference between *intending* and *doing* actually was and messing up that difference had massive consequences.

CHAPTER 9
27th January 2024
Canterbury, England

Zach had been in this particular café plenty of times with Ryan and Lora and some of their other friends, and he had always liked it. The chefs here did the best pizza ever because it was so fresh, so flavourful and the pesto here was to die for. Zach was really glad he had suggested it because after an hour of talking, laughing and smiling about everything and nothing, he was realising why he had been friends with Jayden in the first place.

Zach watched as Jayden finished off his pasta dish with a name he wasn't even going to try to pronounce. It looked cheesy and really nice with chunks of tomatoes, basil and little bowtie pasta shapes. Zach's own dish of Neapolitan pizza had been really delicious with the rich, creamy cheese, rich garlicy tomato sauce and the little touch of basil at the end was a nice touch.

Zach just couldn't believe he was enjoying his time with Jayden so much. He had always been interesting, he had always been caring and he had always been such a nice, wonderful guy that Zach was sort of expecting he was into him a lot more than he wanted to admit.

"Do you mind if I ask you a question about Ryan?" Jayden asked.

Zach froze for a moment so he wrapped his hands round his pint glass of diet coke so it looked like he had been thinking about if he wanted a drink or not.

"Sure," Zach said really not wanting this question to ruin their lunch together.

"What happened? And please know how sorry, so sorry I am for what I did to him," Jayden said.

Zach smiled a little. That was typical Jayden being caring enough to say sorry even though he didn't really know what had happened. Zach had never revealed how much Jayden's question had hurt his ex-boyfriend. Zach had just stopped talking to Jayden before anything else could happen.

Something he was starting to regret.

"What happened?" Jayden asked in a caring and slightly seductive tone that surprised Zach.

Zach was about to answer when a group of students behind him with yellow legal pads started arguing about something. And they had packed up and thankfully left.

That was why Zach hated group projects.

"When you asked Ryan about how he dealt with his parents and family, you freaked him out. It was even worse that you told him I told you about that so he shouted, screamed and he was so mad at me," Zach said.

Zach focused on the bubbles in his Diet Coke as he talked. He didn't want to look at cute Jayden, this was his fault and he should have handled everything better.

"I tried to explain that I had told you a month before and I didn't even expect you to remember. I certainly didn't remember telling you and then he was so mad at me. He actually stayed with Lora for two weeks,"

"Oh shit," Jayden said. "Then what happened because I started to try to get you back after three weeks,"

Zach sighed. He actually wasn't sure what was the worst bit about August and the very early chunk of September. When Jayden had asked the question that had been the first chip in Zach's and Ryan's relationship, or the messages and even a letter trying to get Zach back as his friend.

Zach wasn't sure but that was an intense time.

Zach smiled as he got a whiff of a waiter's apple and rose aftershave with a slight undertone of musk.

"It was okay to be honest for the first week after he came back. We had a lot of sex, he smelt amazing as always with his manly musk and it was nice. Then you started to try to get me back, I tried to hide everything about that from him but he found your letter,"

Zach looked up and he hated seeing how pained Jayden was as he placed his face in his hands with only his sweet eyes visible.

"It was a nice letter by the way, a little long but it was nice hearing what had happened in therapy and why you were the way you were," Zach said.

"But I was silly and intense trying to get you back,"

Zach nodded. "Then me and Ryan had another fight because, I know you are such a cute and nice person. I know you are capable of caring about people so much and you don't know how to process those feelings at times,"

Jayden nodded.

"But Ryan and Lora and everyone doesn't believe me when I say how nice you are and how… I just like you for a reason I don't know or even understand. I just want to be your friend," Zach said.

Zach realised that might have been a little forward but he was really enjoying having lunch with Jayden, a great, cute, attractive man that cared about him. And he had clearly changed for the better.

"I would like to be friends again," Jayden said.

Zach made himself look away for a moment and he focused on the long line of lecturers in their business suits, white shirts and black shoes near the counter. He wanted to be friends again with this cutie.

Zach nodded. "Okay great. But remember, go

slow. We're different people now, you're cute and let's just keep things slow for now,"

"Of course," Jayden said. "But you find me cute?"

Zach just grinned and shook his head because he couldn't confirm that. He found Jayden really cute, attractive and he wanted to do some things to Jayden but he had to protect himself first.

He wanted things to go slow but Zach couldn't deny he wasn't sure he could wait that long. And that was a feeling he hadn't had for a long long time. Maybe since him and Ryan had first met all those long great years ago.

CHAPTER 10
8th February 2024
Canterbury, England

Jayden had absolutely loved the past two weeks with sexy, fit Zach because they had been texting every single day for at least an hour talking about their day, what had happened in the past and just normal friend stuff. Jayden had loved talking with his old best friend and it sort of felt like this was a lot better and healthier than it had been before.

And he flat out loved how light, wonderful and cared for Zach made him feel, but Jayden couldn't deny he was scared as hell about making a mistake. He was always double-checking his messages because he just couldn't afford to sound too intense, too invested and too damaged to Zach.

He couldn't do that again.

"Pass me the eggs please," Caroline said.

Jayden grabbed the six-pack of large eggs on the black chipboard kitchen table that was in Jackie's block of flats. He had never been here before but he rather liked it. The kitchen was massive and Jayden had no idea how many people shared this kitchen, it had to be at least ten or twelve, and everything was black.

Jayden rather liked the smooth black cabinets that were almost posh for university accommodation, the black oven hummed a little louder than he would have liked but he wasn't too concerned, and the bright yellow lights in the ceiling lit up everything perfectly.

The only bad thing about his own flat kitchen was how the lights flickered from time to time. It wasn't meant to but Jayden was just glad modern phones had a torch on them.

He liked the sweet aroma of vanilla, chocolate and mixed spice that filled the kitchen from the cookies and cakes they were baking. He had no idea how the conversation had popped up at first, but he was cooking and that was what he loved doing. Well, he loved it now the girls had strong-armed him into helping out.

"How many cookies are we making?" Jayden asked mixing his own bowl of butter, sugar and flour together.

"I don't know. The University Sports Collective want people to help fundraise for new kit so we are helping," Jackie said.

"It is a little cold in here, don't you think?" Caroline asked adding some vanilla extract to her bowl.

"No, if anything it is way too hot with these ovens on," Katie said.

Jayden just laughed. He had actually been missing his friends lately because instead of spending most evenings with them, he had been texting Zach and he had been working on a bunch of art assignments. He was so glad his drawing was getting better.

"So how's it going with Zach?" Caroline asked readjusting her knitted scarf.

"Really good thanks, but I am a little scared. You know how bad I am with friendships," Jayden said.

"Rubbish," Katie said. "Just because your first friendship with Zach ended in a rather impressive way doesn't mean you're bad at friendships,"

"Sure you can be intense at times," Jackie said. "But we learnt how you work and you learnt how we worked in turn and we love having you as a friend,"

Jayden nodded and he finished mixing up his ingredients and added some mixed spice. He flat out loved the great, rich depth of flavour the brown powder gave his cookies.

He couldn't disagree with his friends though. They were right and he had almost had a fight with Caroline and Katie in the first two months of their friendship because they had accused him of being too intense. And Jayden had argued that he was only being nice, something they agreed to in theory but all the *nice* things Jayden said came out as way too intense.

To the point he made them uncomfortable.

"Why don't you just talk to Zach about your fears?" Katie asked fanning herself with a baking tray.

"Because that's scary and we've only been talking again for another three weeks. It was about this time I started the series of unfortunate events that fucked us up the first time," Jayden said.

He mixed his bowl a little more as his heart rate increased, sweat poured down his back and his ears started ringing.

He forced himself to quietly count out of order but he was tense. He didn't like that fact and now he was just scared he was going to mess everything up like last time.

"Jayden? You okay?" Jackie asked.

Jayden nodded but he was lying. He was not okay. All he wanted in the entire world was to be with, talk to and hug and kiss sexy Zach, but he couldn't. It didn't matter how much he seriously liked Zach, they just couldn't be together because he would mess it up and hurt Zach again and again.

Something he simply could never ever allow.

CHAPTER 11
9th February 2024
Canterbury, England

As much as Zach flat out didn't want to admit it, he couldn't get the idea of Jayden covered in flour, mixed spice and other sweeter things had out of his head. He had no idea he was turned on by the idea of Jayden cooking, but he just wanted to see Jayden again.

And Zach was so impressed that Jayden really had changed because 99% of their messages and conversations were fine. Of course some of Jayden's messages were borderline intense, like how much Jayden cared about him considering they had only reconnected three weeks ago but it was milder than they used to be.

"When am I going to meet your boyfriend?" Lora asked.

Zach laughed to himself as him and Lora went into the bread isle of their local supermarket. He had never been to this one before but it seemed okay, the prices were good, the staff were all fit young men including two Zach had slept with, and the food looked good.

The current isle had a rather interesting (tasteless) black and white diamond tile pattern on it, and the left hand side was lined with some great artisan breads, some commercial ones and some pastries. Zach so badly wanted to buy tons of croissants. They looked great.

Yet Zach was way more interested in the right hand side filled with cakes, cupcakes and an entire range of delicious, creamy, sweet coffee cakes.

"I thought you would like the coffee cakes," Lora said.

Zach stood in front of them and studied them. They looked amazing and the rich aromas of yeast, freshly baked bread and buttery pastries hit his nose, and Zach just knew he was going to be spending a lot of money in this one isle.

"Your new boyfriend when do I get to meet him," Lora said like a child.

"Soon and I think you'll really like him," Zach said.

He wasn't exactly happy he had been lying to Lora for weeks about him texting Jayden, and the one time they had gone out. Yet Jayden was so cute, so funny and just so careful. All Zach wanted to do was look into his strikingly sweet blue eyes again.

Jayden was so, so cute and Zach always felt

brilliant around him.

"Why don't you just tell me who it is?" Lora asked picking up a commercial coffee cake.

"Because I don't want you to scare him off. You're very intense in your protection of me," Zach said knowing the irony there.

"That's only because you let some traumatised loser in your life, he wrecked it and caused you to lose the best relationship you ever had,"

Zach subtly looked at Lora and bit his lip. That wasn't fair, that wasn't right and she was wrong. Jayden was not a loser, he was not a traumatised wreck and he did not ruin anything.

Zach wasn't even sure that Ryan was the love of his life anymore. Sure Ryan was amazing, beautiful and just a God amongst men but he wasn't Jayden. Jayden was so sweet, so caring and so intimate in the non-sexual ways that he didn't actually believe for a moment Ryan was capable of the same.

"Don't you agree?" Lora asked pointing to a more artisan coffee cake.

Zach picked up the smaller but more decorative coffee cake filled with caramelised coated walnuts, and he didn't doubt it was going to bite him in the ass, because this wasn't how he felt but he nodded.

"Yes Jayden did ruin a lot of stuff in my life but he isn't a bad person," Zach said glad he didn't have to lie about the last part.

Lora laughed. "I love you as a friend Zach and I will always protect you,"

Zach smiled his thanks to her and he placed the artisan coffee cake in Lora's basket and they moved onto the bread section. He wasn't exactly a massive fan of bread but he liked sandwiches so they were a necessary evil.

He was really impressed as he looked at the rows upon rows of white, brown and seeded loaves that covered the shelves. It was going to be a nightmare to choose.

"Why don't you like Jayden though?" Zach asked. "Like I know he hurt me so badly and he wrecked Ryan too, but is there anything else?"

"Yeah," Lora said. "I met him once and he's a nice guy but he's just… I don't know. He's pathetic. Like if your life really is as bad as he made out to you then why didn't he fix it sooner?"

Zach tensed a little. That was not a fair question and that was something he always liked about straight people that had lived perfect lives. Lora was a classic straight girl who had had good relationships, had a perfectly supportive family and had never ever been told that being straight was wrong.

Zach hated it how it was pointless trying to tell her about homophobia and how tough life and families could be for queer people. She just believed that because she was really supportive that everyone else was too.

So he went with a classic line that he knew was wasted breath.

"You can only help yourself when you're ready

and you might find me ending the friendship with Jayden gave him the kick he needed to change," Zach said.

"Maybe but he should have done it sooner,"

Zach didn't even comment as he picked up two large packs of croissants and him and Lora went to the checkout.

As much as he loved Lora as a friend, he just wanted to be with Jayden so he was going to invite him out today for a little light lunch.

And that excited Zach way more than he ever wanted to admit.

Little did he realise things were about to start changing. Some good. Some bad.

GAY ROMANCE COLLECTION VOLUME 4

CHAPTER 12
11th February 2024
Canterbury, England

Jayden was so excited that sexy, attractive, fit Zach had asked him out again for a little bit of lunch. He really didn't care what it was, he was just glad to be getting another chance to spend time with him, because texting was great but he just wanted to be with him.

Jayden had to admit as he sat down on the little wooden picnic table that had certainly seen better days (some of the wood had rotten away around the edges) that a picnic lunch might not have been the best idea for February. It was wet, a little chilly and damp.

It might have been right next to a narrow road with a few red, black and green cars parked on one side, but it was private and small. Which Jayden really liked, he loved these small private moments with the man he was falling for, and he never wanted to stop having these moments.

Jayden shivered a little as he got comfortable on the bench of the picnic table but he just couldn't stop looking at Zach as he sat down with a little white tote bag filled with food. Jayden still couldn't believe how artful, fit and divine he looked, and how perfect his body was even with Zach wearing a thin little blue coat.

"Do you remember when we last did this?" Zach asked.

Jayden laughed. "Yeah, me and you were talking one day and Ryan had gone to visit a friend up North so you wanted something to do. And then you of all people convinced me to go painting. I haven't touched watercolours since,"

"You were good though," Zach said getting out a whole host of different picnic pieces.

Jayden smiled to himself. He really liked the croissants, vegan sandwiches, little chocolate eclairs and other things that Zach had brought. It was going to take a while for them to finish this, which was hardly a problem because that just meant he got to spend even more time with the man he was seriously falling for.

"Do you still paint much? And didn't you do puzzles or something?" Jayden asked knowing the answer was yes.

Zach's face lit up and Jayden loved seeing his beautiful, perfect smile that reached all the way up to his eyes.

"Of course, I really like doing puzzles and now I'm back at my uni flat I can spread out on the kitchen table. I have this really beautiful one at the moment that's sort of an abstract photo with stunning, bright colours,"

Jayden reached over and picked up a vegan turkey and stuffing sandwich. He really liked knowing that Zach was still doing what he enjoyed, he was still passionate and he was still excited about a lot of things. And it was so great to hear him talk about his hobbies.

"I would like to see it at some point," Jayden said.

Then he bit his lip because he realised what he was basically asking. He was asking Zach to come to his apartment block, where he lived, studied and slept and that might be a little too soon.

"Relax," Zach said going for Jayden's hand but stopping himself.

Jayden smiled because he so badly wanted Zach to touch him, hold his hand and for something more to happen. And it was a little weird that Zach had gone to touch him, even during their first friendship Zach had never ever done that before.

It was strange and Jayden realised that Zach might actually like him a little more than a friend. It might explain why both of them had been texting each other every single day without fail, and there was interest on both sides. He was wanting to know the ins and outs of Zach's day and Zach would want to know the same for him.

But it was time to stop being a little too cautious.

"Do you like me?" Jayden asked.

His heart pounded in his chest. He didn't want this to be the fuck up moment again. He couldn't keep fucking up friends around the three-week mark.

Zach grinned. "What do you mean *like*? As a friend or more,"

"More," Jayden said.

Zach grabbed a vegan ham and cheese sandwich and Jayden opened his sandwich and he seriously enjoyed the rich, spicy aromas of the vegan turkey and the stuffing that he just knew would be an incredible explosion of flavour on the tongue.

"I think… I think yes I might be into you romantically," Zach said, "because you do make me feel good, I know you're really caring and I have never thought you're a bad guy,"

Jayden didn't know how to take the last part because he wasn't a bad person. He never had been and never ever would be.

"Do you like me?" Zach asked grinning.

"You know I do. I never spoke to you about it when we were friends because you were with Ryan and I respected the hell out of that relationship,"

"And that's why I like you," Zach said liking how Jayden respected his past relationship, "because you're so caring, you're so good and you are really nice,"

Jayden took out the sandwich, surprised by how

incredibly soft the white bread was in his hand.

"So," Jayden said, "do you want to try us dating?"

"Aren't we already?" Zach asked grinning. "We text daily, we go out and we both like each other's company,"

"Maybe we are," Jayden said but he so badly wanted to say so much more and he couldn't believe how brilliant this lunch was.

All he wanted to do was hug, kiss and hold Zach's hand, but he forced himself not to. Zach had only agreed to date and this was the start of a new relationship. They had technically only been dating ten seconds, but Jayden felt like he had been dating and being with Zach in his mind for weeks.

Jayden was about to say something when he saw someone out of the corner of his eye.

"What the hell are you two doing?" Ryan asked.

Jayden's stomach churned up a storm as he realised his nice peaceful lunch was going to end badly.

CHAPTER 13
11th February 2024
Canterbury, England

Zach flat out didn't understand what was happening as he watched Ryan with his sensational body storm over to him and Jayden as they sat at the picnic table. He had picked this spot at the university because it was isolated, private and perfect for a date in all but name.

Zach just looked at how great Ryan looked with his sensational biceps, six-pack abs and insanely fit body as his tight-fitting black hoody and jeans left little to the imagination.

"What the hell are you two doing?" Ryan asked.

Zach didn't need this. He had only wanted to have a nice lunch with a friend who he really, really liked. He didn't want any drama, any pain or trouble, and he certainly didn't want to see his ex-boyfriend.

He placed the vegan ham and cheese sandwich back in the packet because as much as he wanted to enjoy the extreme creaminess of the cheese, he simply had to deal with this first.

"We're having lunch together and it isn't any of your business who I spend time with," Zach said knowing it was a complete and utter lie because of who Jayden was.

Ryan stopped right next to Zach and Zach forced himself not to smile as Ryan's thick manly musk hit his nose and made his wayward parts spring to life. Ryan must have just finished football practice or something so he would be hot, sweaty and horny as always.

"Do you not know what *that* boy did to me? To us? He is a hurtful, self-fish, intense idiot. They are your words, not mine and you are spending time with him," Ryan said.

Zach didn't dare look at Jayden. He didn't know what he would say because Ryan was right, he had said a lot of nasty stuff about Jayden in the weeks after he had ended their friendship.

"And how long has this been happening? And most importantly why the hell would you let that loser back into your life after what he did to you, to me and our relationship? Did you ever end the friendship?"

Zach just looked straight into Ryan's eyes. "Of course I bloody did. I ended my friendship with him, because he was too intense, he was a nightmare and he was toxic back then. He's better now and healthier,"

Ryan laughed and looked at Jayden. Zach had no

idea what either one of them were thinking, he wanted to spare Jayden some pain and make up some half-truth about what had happened behind closed doors but he couldn't.

Ryan wanted to have this fight and he was going to have it now of all times.

"You called you every word under the sun you know," Ryan said grinning. "You called you pathetic, weak, a wreck and everything else. He doesn't care about you. You're a charity case, a nothing and you never will be anything,"

Zach was about to say something when Ryan walked away and Zach found some strength to stand up.

"You ended you and me you know. And I only started talking to Jayden three weeks ago. That's the truth,"

He never had expected Ryan to turn around and respond but it still hurt that he didn't. Zach had never wanted to hurt anyone and Ryan had been a great boyfriend who cared and treasured Zach a lot, but Zach couldn't really understand why Ryan had never forgiven Zach for telling Jayden things about his life.

Zach could understand the things he had told Jayden in an effort to help him were never his things to share, but that wasn't a reason to hate him for months and then dump him. Not after Zach had done a million things to make it up to him.

"Are you okay?" Jayden asked.

Zach laughed as he looked at the cute, innocent

man that he had always cared so much about. It was why he had listened and allowed Jayden to basically shit all over him about his mental health, how bad his life was and how bad his family was.

Because Zach really, really cared about Jayden. He was so cute, so sweet and so perfect in every way and even now, Jayden was still focusing on others.

He was so amazing.

"No not really," Zach said. "I didn't want to hurt Ryan and I didn't want to hurt you,"

Jayden gestured he wanted to reach across the table and hold Zach's hand, which Zach allowed. They both grinned like schoolboys as they enjoyed the warmth, attraction and sexual chemistry that flowed between them.

Zach gently rubbed Jayden's hand. "I am sorry you know about what I said,"

Jayden tensed. "You didn't have to confirm it,"

"I didn't want to lie to you. It all mattered but I was so angry and mad at myself, Ryan and what had happened to our relationship that… I regret a lot of things I said about you,"

"Do you still think of me like that?"

"Never," Zach said picking up his ham and cheese sandwich again. "I like you a lot so let's try to move on. Let's focus on the future, do you want that?"

"I really would," Jayden said as he finished off his own sandwich and moaned in pleasure at the taste.

Zach just hoped beyond hope Jayden would one

day moan at him in utter pleasure because he loved that sound and he really wanted to hear it over and over again.

CHAPTER 14
11th February 2024
Canterbury, England

As much as Jayden didn't want to admit it, he couldn't help but have Ryan's cold, hard words replay constantly in his head. He was helping Caroline (who was now wearing three scarves because it was apparently too damn cold), Jackie and Katie (who was wearing blue shorts and a tank top because it was too warm on an icy cold February late afternoon).

Jayden really didn't understand his friends' temperature sensitivities at times, but he loved them, supported them and considering he had ditched them to hang out with Zach, he sort of owed them.

Jayden had two large plastic boxes filled with about a hundred largeish chocolate chip cookies. The rich butter, sugar and dark chocolate hints that filled his senses made Jayden really want to chomp into the box himself, but Jackie had made a plate of cookies for the four of them so sadly he was going to have to wait.

Even though he seriously didn't want to.

Jayden really liked the main plaza of the campus, where the Sports Guild wanted everyone to leave their donations. Jayden had always liked how large it was so three rows of exotic food trucks could line up and serve students. Today it seemed like the local Indian, Chinese and Japanese food trucks dominated the scene.

Jayden had always preferred when the middle eastern trucks were there but hopefully they would be back tomorrow or sometime soon.

"What is that smell?" Caroline asked loudly.

Jayden laughed as he looked over to the coffee shop next to university bookshop with beautiful, breath-taking displays of the latest bestsellers and the local corner shop on the very end.

He coughed a few times as the coffee shop had clearly burnt their coffee beans yet again. It was so overwhelming, so awful and so strange that Jayden was definitely going to get out of here as soon as possible.

"That coffee shop's always burning their bean," Jackie said as she carried three boxes of cookies.

Jayden followed the women as they all made their way towards the large white tent in the middle of the plaza with a long line of students with their own donations.

Something he had no intention of waiting for.

"Hey," Katie said, "didn't you say you saw Ryan

earlier?"

"Yeah why?" Jayden asked.

"Isn't that his boyfriend Colin?" Katie asked gesturing with her head to the white tent.

Jayden just rolled his eyes and frowned. Of course it was bloody Colin up ahead taking all the donations, writing up what was what and smiling and being all friendly when in reality he was a dickhead.

Zach had only told him what had happened at the Big Fair about a week into them restarting their friendships. Jayden had wanted to say some strong words but he behaved himself.

He flat out couldn't believe that Colin would actually shoved the fact he was Ryan's new boyfriend in Zach's face. Who did that? Especially considering how much Zach had been hurting at the time.

"You alright?" Caroline asked.

Jayden smiled at her. "I don't know,"

And then Jayden told them all about what Ryan had said to him about Zach's choice words when their friendship had ended.

"He was angry," Jackie said flicking the plastic boxes up because they were clearly getting too heavy for her.

"I guess so but if he really cared about me back then, why would he say it?" Jayden asked.

"Dearest," Caroline said shivering slightly, "you know how much we love you but you ever think, you and Zach are living too much in the past,"

Jayden shrugged. He had no idea what the hell

she was talking about, but Jayden couldn't help himself when he realised how great the light was with the cold grey sky above with but small rays of golden sunlight still managed to light up the sky.

It was only now Jayden was realising just how much he had been neglecting his passion, his favourite hobby and the thing that had gotten him through so much. He definitely needed to go on an "artist date" again to just take photos.

And enjoy his favourite artform.

Jayden stepped out the way of a student as a large group of them walked past.

"Answer the question," Jackie said smiling.

"I don't know Jackie," Jayden said. "You have no idea what it was like to have a breakdown, lose someone who you had a toxic and very unhealthy relationship with and then have to recover from that,"

The women went silent and then Caroline wrapped her scarves a little tighter and smiled.

"I'm sorry, we don't know what it was like," Caroline said. "We only know the aftermath and how much you struggled during those four months when you were trying to get back on your feet,"

"But," Jackie said, "we also know how great you are, how caring you are and how much Zach means to you now. Maybe just see if you can let go of the past, hurt and anything that happened between you both,"

Jayden smiled. "If I wasn't holding these boxes I would hug you all,"

"Then let's put down our boxes," Katie said.

Jayden put down his boxes at the same time his friends did and then they all did a massive group hug, because they were right. He should talk to Zach about just forgetting and not worrying about the past.

They were different people now and he was healthier, stronger and he wasn't dependent or intense with Zach anymore. He knew what to say and what not to say to people.

And the very idea of that made Jayden so damn excited because it meant there could be a real wonderful, lovely chance of him and Zach having a relationship that was healthy and not wrapped up in the past.

A past that was extremely hurtful and damaging for both of them.

Little did Jayden realise everything was about to come crashing down.

CHAPTER 15
17th February 2024
Canterbury, England

Now Zach definitely knew how Jayden had felt when he had asked him out that one time to do painting in the woods where both of them lived, the idea of an "artist date" sounded silly, a little weird and a little woo-woo. But if it meant spending time with someone as fit, hot and attractive as Jayden then he was up for it.

Which was probably the exact same reason Jayden had agreed to go painting with him.

"This is beautiful and perfect for painting," Jayden said.

Zach just grinned as him and Jayden walked through Blean Wood. The air was cold, damp and crisp so there might not have been much mud but the ground was lumpy and uneven. Not that Zach minded too much.

He had always wanted to go to Blean Woods

near Kent University but he had never had the time to go yet. And now he was here with the man he was seriously falling for, he was so damn happy that he had come here.

Zach was rather impressed with the thin silver birch, pine and oak trees that lined the pathway. Their branches were shooting out in all directions and long blanche vines hung off some of the trees.

"Oh wow. That is so perfect," Jayden said as he knelt down, messed around with angling his professional camera and he took a few shots.

Zach laughed, because Jayden was so damn cute. He had no idea what Jayden saw in the Woods, it was a complete mystery to him but he loved, truly loved seeing Jayden so happy and in his element.

When Jayden came over to him and showed him some of his photos, Zach was amazed at how detailed the photos of a Robin were in the trees. The detail in the photo was only amplified by the lighting, the slight sparkle on the branch because of the frost being hit by the sunlight at just the right angle.

"You're amazing you know," Zach said.

Jayden grinned. "Um, I really want to kiss you,"

Zach smiled and he honestly couldn't have cared less that he was technically in public and Jayden had said back in August that he would never kiss another man in public.

Zach took a step closer and he gently stroked Jayden's cheek with one hand and he ran the other hand down his black coat.

He liked it when Jayden's breath caught and Zach went closer.

When their lips met, Zach moaned in pleasure as Jayden did the same. The kiss was electric, intense and so tender and filled with so much passion that Zach never ever wanted this kiss to end.

This was so much better than anything Ryan had ever given him because this was a deep, intense, caring kiss. It wasn't a hot, I-want-to-fuck-you kiss, this was a you-matter-so-much-to-me kiss.

And Zach loved it.

"Wow," Jayden said. "Thank you,"

Zach playfully hit him on the arm and he took Jayden's hand in his as they went along the pathway. Whilst trying not to twist an ankle on the uneven ground.

"You know when I see something picture worthy I'm going to let go," Jayden said grinning.

Zach ignored it. "You don't have to thank me for kissing you. I like you a lot and, I meant what I said about wanting to give us a try now you're better and healthier,"

Jayden looked around. "Thanks, and you know I am so sorry for what happened before,"

"I know," Zach said meaning it. "You were just trying to deal with a bad situation at home, you were trying to do it all alone and you just developed an unhealthy attachment to me because I was the only person that accepted you,"

"And you're beautiful," Jayden said.

"Getting intense again," Zach said with a small smile.

"Sorry," Jayden said as he let go and knelt down to take another photo of something in the trees.

"See but I like this, this is what we need to do. Just be open, talk and just you make a mistake I'll correct you and you can do the same with me,"

"Now that I would like. Definitely going to make talking to you less stressful for me," Jayden said.

"And that's what boyfriends are for,"

Zach stopped dead in his tracks as soon as the words left his mouth. The term *boyfriend* felt strange, awkward and a little weird to say out loud. He had called Ryan his boyfriend for more years than he cared to admit so it felt a little weird calling Jayden of all people his boyfriend.

But he couldn't help but smile because it felt good, right and lovely to call him his boyfriend.

"One of my friends mentioned something a few days ago," Jayden said. "She thinks both of us are living too much in the past,"

Zach nodded and he jogged a little to catch up with Jayden who was already taking more photos of something up ahead.

He supposed that was sort of fair. Both of them had been concerned about how the other would react because of what had happened before, so maybe they should forget the past and just live in the moment. And if something connected to the past popped up then they would deal with it.

So that's exactly what Zach told him.

Jayden hugged him and Zach liked the feeling of his hard body against his.

"Actually," Jayden said. "When we went painting that time I really wanted a photo of us together. Can I… I don't know, have one now?"

"Sure but how can you take a selfie on that pro cam of yours. Does it have a secret selfie setting?" Zach asked failing to stop himself from laughing.

Jayden playfully hit Zach on the head. "No I have a phone for that,"

Zach went over to Jayden and they both placed a tight, caring arm around each other, they grinned and they both took some pictures.

Zach poked his tongue out on some of them. They both pulled silly faces and then there were nice ones and happy ones and photos that just made Zach want to cry in happiness. He loved this. He loved these small precious moments where they could be a real couple without worrying what others would say about them.

Lora was still banging on about how he was hiding something and Ryan had been messaging him on social media. Ryan was threatening him, telling him he was making a big mistake and Zach had tried blocking him but Ryan just had a new account.

"Want to think about going back?" Jayden asked after they took a final couple's photo together. "It's early, we can catch a film or something at my flat,"

Zach laughed and he was about to respond when

he heard a twig snap in the distance.

"Seriously!" Lora shouted. "This is your boyfriend. What the fuck!"

Zach's eyes widened as he realised shit was about to hit the fan.

CHAPTER 16
17th February 2024
Canterbury, England

Jayden flat out couldn't believe what was happening here. It couldn't be her, not Lora. Anything but that woman with her long angelic blond hair that had made his life hell back in September and October when he had seen her a few times.

Not Lora. She was evil, harsh and an awful person who hated him.

Jayden felt his heart pound in his chest, cold sweat ran back down his back and his ears rang slightly as he watched as her and Ryan come down the path towards them. The uneven frozen ground didn't even seem to slow them or bother them in the slightest.

The pine, oaks and silver birches moved slightly and their branches banged into each other as an icy cold breeze flew through the woodlands. And Jayden just knew that this was going to end badly.

"So this is your boyfriend?" Lora asked frowning.

"I wasn't lying to you," Zach said. "I just sort of bent the truth because Jayden wasn't my boyfriend when we first started talking,"

"How bloody long has this been happening?" Lora asked.

Jayden shivered at the rage and anger and hate in her voice. He hadn't realised Lora still had so much hate in her after she had cornered him in one of the shops on campus and really bit into him.

Jayden had cried so damn much that evening and he had done everything he could to forget it.

Ryan stepped forward. "See Lora Zach doesn't care about you. You were always a good friend to me after what that loser did to me and Zach, but Zach just doesn't care. He only ever thinks of himself,"

"Shut up," Jayden said. "You're a snake and you just hate me for going what you went through,"

"No," Ryan said taking a few steps closer to him. "I hate you because you are a loser, a charity case and you are nothing,"

Jayden forced back the tears. It was happening all over again but instead of happening over text, it was happening to his face.

"Enough," Zach said. "Me and Jayden are trying to date and I was going to tell you and-"

"He's only going to hurt you or have you actually forgotten what that loser did to you and Ryan back in August?" Lora asked.

Jayden couldn't help but look at Zach. He had

always known he had hurt Zach with his intensity, his obsessiveness and his sharp questions about how to cope with his trauma and abuse but he had never wanted to know *just* how much he had hurt him.

The man he seriously liked and cared for and maybe even loved.

The dampness in the air got even thicker as Jayden realised that Zach was looking at the ground. He might have been thinking or remembering and Jayden really wanted to support him.

Surely that was how good relationships were formed, one partner supporting the other partner and then their relationship got even stronger and better. That was how it worked, surely?

Jayden took a few steps forward. "You might not like me but I do love Zach and I genuinely care about him. I won't hurt him again and I'm better now,"

"No you aren't," Zach said looking up at Jayden with watery eyes.

Lora and Ryan laughed and Jayden shivered as he hated the sound of that cackling.

"You have only known me again for three weeks. You can't *love* me," Zach said straining to keep back the tears. "You are so intense, so connected to feelings that it takes others time to develop and you… you are so lovely but I can't keep doing this. Every time you come into my life you cause so much upheaval,"

Jayden's eyes widened. It was happening. He had fucked-up yet again because he had been too intense, he had said those little words too soon and Zach didn't feel the same.

He was an idiot.

"So… so you're siding with them?" Jayden asked pointing to Lora and Ryan.

Zach shook his head. "You all pretend to care about me but Lora you just want to control me. You could have asked and respected my decision to talk to Jayden again. And Ryan stop texting and threatening me,"

Jayden was about to say something and question that but Zach just glared at him.

"You are so caring and kind but, I just can't keep doing this with you," Zach said as he walked away.

Jayden looked at Ryan and Lora as they looked all nice and smug and Jayden stood his ground. He didn't need to be scared of them anymore, he didn't need to be concerned about what they thought of him, he didn't even like them.

When Zach was out of sight Ryan and Lora smiled and bowed and walked away.

"Loser," Ryan said.

Lora turned around. "And you do realise, it was only a week ago Zach said *Jayden ruined a lot of stuff in my life,*"

Jayden didn't dare react until they were out of sight and then he simply fell against an icy cold oak tree and he let everything out.

All his pain. All his anger. All his sadness.

It all came out.

CHAPTER 17
17th February 2024
Canterbury, England

Zach had absolutely no idea if it had been forecasted to rain later in the day but he hadn't checked. He continued along a long road filled with potholes and wonderful little semi-detached houses with white exteriors, perfectly clean driveways and little rose gardens out front as he went back towards the university.

The rain fell down all around him and Zach just smiled for a moment because his coat was thin, so it was good for warmth in the cold but it was useless in the rain. Especially heavy rain like this one.

A black car drove past him with its headlights on as the grey sky started to turn a little black. Even three of the streetlamps turned on as Zach went past because it was so dark like his mood.

Zach was slightly regretting finding a park bench to sit down for a long time (he had no idea how long he had sat there just hating his life and hating everything about Ryan) because now he was caught in the rain and he was going to get soaked.

Zach was surprised how deafening the rain was as it splashed onto the pavement, it hit tin roofs of little outbuildings in people's gardens and cars past him.

This really wasn't how he had wanted today to go but he had sort of always known this was what would happen in the end.

He had always known that Jayden "loved" him and Zach wanted to joke to himself that it was impossible not to. Jayden had always liked blonds and men with fit bodies and Zach supposed he was very good in both departments.

He had just never wanted Jayden to be so intense in that particular moment. Not when Ryan and Lora were there with him or against him as was the case. Zach had really wanted Jayden to be quiet and maybe he could have reasoned with his friend and ex so they would leave him alone.

Zach shivered as his hair was soaking wet, his coat wasn't doing anything anymore to keep the water out and the light cold breeze was starting to chill him. He still had another five, ten minutes easily before he reached the university and then another ten minutes of walking before he reached his shared flat.

It wasn't ideal but nothing about today was.

Zach couldn't really blame Jayden though because he knew he had only been trying to help.

Jayden was probably trying to be the same lovely, caring and wonderful person that he always had been. He probably saw the situation with Lora and Ryan as a problem that needed to be fixed and he wanted to try.

He was great like that.

Zach smiled to himself as he kept walking through the rain because he really did like Jayden.

Zach had never really meant something as kind, caring and great as Jayden. Because sure Jayden could be intense as hell at times, it was wrong of him to say he loved Zach after only three weeks, but Jayden had never been a bad person.

And Zach wasn't sure he wanted a repeat of the past.

He had never really given it much thought before now because he had been so focused on Ryan and angry at Jayden. But it had sort of killed him the first time he had put his friendship on pause with Jayden.

He wasn't sure why he felt like someone had ripped out a part of him, but now he supposed it was because Jayden had been such a good, lovely and fun friend for that month.

They had talked a lot, gone out a lot and they were always smiling and laughing and having fun. And Zach had hated putting the friendship on pause because that meant all the "fun" just stopped immediately.

He regretted that now.

Zach shivered again as the rain came down even

harder and he was fairly sure he looked like a drowned rat with his blond hair being darkened and awful.

He was so cold and shaking. He just wanted to go home back to his apartment.

Zach tried to get his phone now so he could text one of his flatmates to put the kettle on and make sure the heating in the shared kitchen was on, that radiator was bigger so he could dry more of his clothes, but his hands were shaking too badly to do anything.

He was so cold.

Zach saw a large white SUV drive up next to him before it sped up and drove right through a puddle.

It splashed all over him and Zach just wanted to cry. This day wasn't going right but he wasn't going to let the past repeat itself.

He cared and seriously liked Jayden so he was going to go to his shared university accommodation and get warm there and sort this out.

Mainly because he didn't want to lose Jayden but also because Jayden's accommodation was so much closer than his own.

And right now he only wanted to get warm and he seriously wanted to get warm in Jayden's arms.

CHAPTER 18
17th February 2024
Canterbury, England

Jayden was rather impressed with himself for not spending any more than twenty minutes crying, screaming and just being angry at himself, the world and Lora (with Ryan just being a natural idiot). He was even happier he had managed to make it back to his university accommodation before the rain had started.

"I hope Caroline doesn't melt out there," Katie said fanning herself.

Jayden smiled to himself as he wrapped his hands round the piping hot mug of coffee that Jackie had made him.

They were all sitting in Jayden's shared kitchen and Jayden was just glad it was so clean for a change. He had never seen the black fake-marble countertops so clean, shiny and they smelt of orange-scented bleach. That wasn't a bad smell at all. Jayden was impressed the other flatmates had really been brilliant about their cleaning responsibilities after the university had moaned and officially warned them yesterday.

Even the black chipboard dining table that had more cracks and holes than most UK roads was rather impressive. Jayden could almost see his own reflection in it but Jayden seriously doubted Caroline would melt.

"She isn't a witch you know," Jayden said.

"How do you know? She's always cold and the rain only makes things colder," Katie said grinning. "Maybe she's cold blooded,"

Jayden almost jumped at the deafening sound of the rain hammering into the glass windows of the kitchen that was only amplified by the echoing in the kitchen. He really hoped the rain would lighten up soon.

Jackie took a few sips of her herbal tea and shook her head.

"I'm sorry about what happened," Jackie said before looking at Katie. "Because someone here needs to be supportive,"

"I was going to comfort him but I was more concerned about Caroline and I hate this heating by the way,"

Jayden smiled. He really did love his friends.

"Do you think you'll contact him again?" Jackie asked like how a mother might ask a small child something.

Jayden shrugged. "Yeah probably, but not for a few days. Part of the reason why Zach put our friendship on pause in the first time was because I was contacting Ryan too much in an effort to become friends with him,"

Katie went round the table and hugged Jayden. "I am so proud of you,"

"Why?" Jayden asked.

Jackie looked like it was obvious. "Because that's healthy. It means you can learn from your mistakes and you want to get better at friendships and relationships,"

Jayden nodded. That was fair and he really wanted Zach to know he was different, he was healthy and he was committed to trying to be a good boyfriend.

"But how are you doing?" Katie asked taking a seat at the table.

"I don't know to be honest. It was so... weird seeing Lora again because I hadn't seen her since the start of the year,"

"What happened and why didn't you tell us?" Katie asked. "You've known us all since September,"

Jayden just looked at his steaming coffee. "Because after everything with Zach I convinced myself that talking about how I was wasn't a good thing. I didn't want to burden you and our friendships were way too new for that sort of information,"

Katie looked like she was going to say something but Jackie just glared at her.

"Maybe you're right and me and Katie don't have to think about the same things as you when it comes to friendships,"

Katie nodded like that was what she had always wanted to say.

Jayden was about to say something because he felt great and he had always liked how wonderful Zach made him feel, but the rain got even louder and he could barely hear himself think over the noise of the rain against the window.

Then it went quiet for a moment before the rain continued to hammer down and echo around the kitchen.

"I miss him," Jayden said. "I really miss Zach and I don't want him to be angry with me. I didn't mean to hurt him, and don't, want him to go through what he went through in August,"

Jackie and Katie smiled like they knew something.

Jayden took a sip of his strong bitter coffee and gestured them to say whatever they wanted, he really hoped it was going to be helpful.

"Then you wait a few days, prove you aren't intense and obsessive like before and then you fight for this relationship," Jackie said. "You go slow to continue to prove how much better you are and then you convince Zach through your actions that this relationship matters,"

Jayden nodded. He liked the idea of that because all he wanted in the entire world was to see Zach's fit, sexy body again and amazing smile. Jayden wanted to kiss Zach's soft, wonderful lips again and he really wanted to run his fingers through Zach's delightfully soft blond hair.

Zach was so beautiful and perfect and Jayden's stomach filled with butterflies.

He got what he said was wrong and he shouldn't have said he loved Zach so soon, but he really, really did.

The kitchen door opened and Jayden's mouth dropped and he couldn't help but grin as Caroline came in (soaking wet) with some blond man that looked like a drowned rat.

The most beautiful drowned rat Jayden had ever seen.

CHAPTER 19
17th February 2024
Canterbury, England

Zach was so damn cold and he couldn't stop his shivering as he stood in the doorway to Jayden's shared kitchen. He was glad Jayden had mentioned where to find his flat and accommodation in passing in a random conversation they had been having over text, because he was so damn cold.

He really liked it how Jayden came over to him and hugged him and gently pulled himself inside. Zach just grinned because he knew that Jayden was going to take good care of him and then when he was thawed out Zach really hoped they could sort everything out.

As Jayden focused on getting him out of his soaking wet coat, Zach wanted to cough at the sheer strength of the cloves, oranges and lemon aromas in the air. Maybe it was from bleach or something because the kitchen was so clean but it was strong.

Too strong for it to be normal.

The sheer strength of the aromas made Zach's eyes water and his body kept shivering. He had never seen countertops so shiny and clean and black, and the dining table that looked like it was going to fall apart at any moment looked relatively new (from a secondhand store).

"Tea or coffee?" the woman who called herself Caroline asked.

Zach tried to talk but his teeth were chattering too much. He hated being this cold and wet but he loved it when Jayden hugged him tight after putting his coat on the radiator near the window.

Zach hugged Jayden as tight as he could manage as he shook. And he realised if someone walked past they might have thought he was twerking on Jayden, he was shivering so badly.

Zach gasped as Jayden playfully put his wonderfully warm hands under Zach's wet hoody and he grinned like a little schoolboy. He was even happier that Jayden didn't stop and Zach laughed and his wayward parts sprung to life as Jayden explored his body.

"I knew you were fit but I didn't realise you had such a hard body," Jayden said like he was a kid in a candy store.

"Here's your coffee," Caroline said clearly choosing Zach's drink for herself.

Zach clung to Jayden a little as they went over to the dining table with two other women already sitting around it. He had no idea why one of the women were wearing shorts and a tank top on such a cold day so she had to be Katie.

"Are you okay enough to come into my room and change?" Jayden asked. "Just to get you into some new clothes, I promise I can wait outside whilst you change and we don't have to talk or anything until you go back,"

Zach rubbed his hands together and he wrapped them round his wonderfully warm coffee mug. He smiled at Jayden for a moment because Lora was so wrong about Jayden. He had changed, he was different and he was a lot more aware of his intensity at times.

Of course Jayden would make mistakes but Zach knew he wasn't exactly perfect either. But he still wanted him and Jayden to work out so that was why he was here.

"I appreciate it you know," Zach said grinning. "It means a lot that you're trying but I wouldn't mind getting out of my clothes, and you can watch if you want,"

Zach was so glad he was sitting down as his wayward parts were showing as clear as day to see in his soaking wet jeans.

"I wouldn't mind that either," Jayden said as they both got up, took their mugs with them and they both said bye to the girls.

Zach followed Jayden out along a narrow little corridor with dirty white walls and the same blue carpet squares that the university seemed to be obsessed with.

Then Jayden opened a door and they went into his flat. Zach was impressed with it, it was rather lovely, small but lovely. He smiled at the rather beautiful photos hanging on the walls, he knew he shouldn't have been but he was always surprised at how great of a photographer Jayden was.

The bed was small, a little high and Zach wasn't sure if he was going to have to jump up to get on it, but that was definitely a theory to test later on.

Jayden pushed past him to get to a small wardrobe and Zach watched as Jayden expertly picked out a matching black outfit of a black hoody, jogging bottoms and a black t-shirt. Zach had wanted to ask for some boxer briefs so he could get out of his soaking wet underwear but he supposed he wanted to keep Jayden guessing about some stuff in their relationship.

"Here you go," Jayden said weakly smiling as he passed the clothes to Zach. "I am sorry you know,"

Zach nodded. "I know you are and that's why I'm here. Stand over there, watch me get changed if you want and we'll talk because I think there's a lot we need to fix before we can be together,"

"Like what?" Jayden asked, "you make it sound like there's more to fix than you and me,"

Zach nodded because as much as he didn't want to admit it, he did want his best friend back.

"I know it sounds stupid but Lora is a great

friend and she cares about me a lot. If there's a chance we can still be friends and if she can accept you're a good part of my life then I want to take it. Is that okay?"

Zach wasn't sure what Jayden was going to say for a moment but after a few seconds, he nodded.

"If that helps you to be happy then that's okay and we all need more friends these days,"

Zach hugged him. Jayden really was brilliant, caring and wonderful and he was so glad he had come here to fix everything.

Now he just needed to get out of these soaking clothes and get warm.

CHAPTER 20
17th February 2024
Canterbury, England

Jayden had absolutely no idea what he needed to do in this situation as he leant against a warm white wall of his flat. He watched a very hot, fit and soaking wet Zach place the clothes down on his bed and Zach stood in the narrow gap between his desk and his bed.

Jayden had always wanted to see Zach's fit, attractive and just divine body under his clothes but he had never thought he was actually going to see it. Especially with Zach shaking and shivering so much from the cold.

All Jayden wanted to do was go over to Zach and brush his soaking wet hair to one side and just kiss him and love him.

"You nervous?" Zach asked as he took his drenched hoody and damp t-shirt off.

"Maybe," Jayden said.

Jayden couldn't help but grin like an idiot as he admired Zach's insanely fit body. He had always known there were no muscles and no real definition to Zach's body but it was still amazing to look at. There wasn't an ounce of body fat, Zach had a strong stomach line and his body curved slightly so Jayden was certain if Zach did some ab workouts he would have a six-pack in a short order.

He was that fit.

Jayden was surprised when Zach didn't put on his dry hoody and t-shirt. Instead Zach took off his soaking wet jeans and Jayden gasped in pleasure.

Zach's legs were long, sexy and thin like he had always known. They were hairless and smooth and Jayden really wanted to run a hand up them and Zach's package was hardly a bad side.

And Zach was clearly aroused to say the least.

Then Jayden crossed his own legs as Zach got unchanged into Jayden's favourite black hoody, jogging bottoms and t-shirt.

"That was very nice. Thanks for that," Jayden said.

"You're welcome I want to see your body at some point too,"

Jayden laughed and shook his head because this was why he had always loved him and Zach. Their friendship and relationship was so fun, full of laughter and it was so positive.

"Help me up," Zach said as he tried jumping up on Jayden's bed but he couldn't.

Jayden hugged and lifted up Zach and he accidentally threw him on the bed and then Jayden sat next to him.

"Note to self you throwing me on the bed is hot," Zach said like he was embarrassed.

"So we're okay then?"

"Yeah. I think we always were okay but I was just shocked that you said *I love you* and there was all the grief from Ryan and Lora and I just needed some space,"

Jayden took Zach's hand in his. "I know I can be a lot at times and I know the intensity of emotions isn't normal, but I am trying. Just ask the girls because I have been intense with them before and I am a lot better now,"

Zach nodded. "I know, over the past three weeks I know you've been a lot better and not *as* intense. Sure you're going to make mistakes at times because you are intense and that's partly why I like you so much,"

Jayden smiled. His stomach filled with butterflies at the idea of Zach liking him a lot.

"And I know," Zach said, "I can't change how intense you feel things, but I can tell you and help you come across as less intense. Like if we're talking and you get intense then I'll just tell you and we make a course correction or something. Is that okay?"

Jayden nodded and hugged Zach.

"That was all I ever wanted in the first place," Jayden said. "When you put us on pause and when I was trying to get you back, I know I was super intense and maybe even a little unstable back then, but you only had to talk to me."

"Yeah, um sorry,"

"It's okay," Jayden said breaking the hug and running his hand through Zach's damp hair.

"Let's just promise from now on we'll start talking more, we'll focus on being us and supporting each other. Because I want this relationship to work,"

"Me too," Jayden said.

Jayden loved it how Zach pulled him close and kissed him again. Jayden couldn't believe how great and soft and wonderful Zach's lips felt against his and he never wanted this moment to end.

It was perfect.

"You want to watch something and snuggle?" Zach asked.

Jayden nodded and grinned like a schoolboy as he grabbed his laptop and snuggled with the beautiful man he loved.

He knew that they still needed to fix Zach's and Lora's friendship and deal with Ryan but tonight was about them. And that made Jayden a lot more excited than he had been in his entire life.

And that was a great feeling to have.

CHAPTER 21
24th February 2024
Canterbury, England

Zach was flat out shocked that he had to take a leaf out of Jayden's book when it came to Lora, because Zach had wanted to text her, phone her and fix everything about their friendship the day after she had almost wrecked his relationship with the man he loved. But Zach couldn't believe that Jayden had been right that he should wait a few more days, maybe a week and then approach Lora.

Now Zach knew exactly how Jayden felt when he had paused their friendship, even though this was slightly different.

About a week later, Zach held the hand of the beautiful man he loved as they both sat down in the library café at a small plastic table with a horribly wobbly leg, as they saw Lora coming towards them.

The entire café with its white walls, massive floor-to-ceiling windows and tons upon tons of students revising with their friends made Zach smile a little. He had never liked coming to the library café because he just wasn't comfortable and he had always revised better in his room. If he wanted to see his friends he would go out with them, he seriously wouldn't revise or study with them.

"You okay?" Jayden asked.

Zach laughed. "You're always asking about me. Shouldn't I be asking you about how you're feeling, after all Lora did shout at you a few times?"

As much as Zach had loved spending the past week kissing, hugging and watching films with Jayden, he had hated to find out what Lora had done behind his back. Even when he was so annoyed at Jayden for his intensity and emotional dependency, she never should have shouted or cornered him.

That was wrong.

"Thanks for the coffee," Lora said sitting down on the chair opposite them.

Zach smiled at his old best friend. Lora looked really well and she was sipping the coffee they had brought her so she clearly wasn't *that* angry at them.

Zach squeezed Jayden's wonderfully smooth, soft hand a little. He hated Jayden to start talking but Lora was his friend so this was his problem to solve.

"I'm sorry Zach didn't tell you about us," Jayden said. "I never wanted that and I've actually always liked how good you two are as friends,"

Lora took a sip of her coffee. "Thanks because unlike you I don't hurt Zach and I always look out for him,"

"You're hurting me right now," Zach said.

Zach had never expected to say it but he was only realising how he had been spending the past week, and every waking moment with the man he loved, because he didn't want to be alone so he could think about how badly his friend had treated him.

"What do you mean?" Lora asked. "I am only looking out for you, it's what I have always done,"

"You have done nothing but-" Zach said.

"I think you mean that," Jayden said, "but I think you're going about it the wrong way because you are hurting his feelings,"

Zach was surprised Jayden could speak so calmly, nicely and like Lora actually had a good point. Maybe he didn't need to fix this problem alone.

"I think," Jayden said, "you want to know about me and if there is any chance I am going to hurt Zach again like I did before,"

Lora played with her coffee cup and nodded a little. Zach was glad to see she was calmer now with the rich bitter aroma of the coffee filling the air and she leant forward so she had to be listening to Jayden. There was clearly a first time for everything.

"I have been through therapy, I have been through a lot of personal growth with my friends that I have now and I am a lot better. I've dealt with my past really well and I'm dealing with everything that pops up,"

"Okay," Lora said playing with her coffee cup

even more making the aroma of coffee even more intense, "but can you promise without a shadow of a doubt you will never hurt him again?"

Zach looked at the man he loved and smiled, because it was a pointless question. They were a couple in love, they liked each other a lot and Zach just knew there might be arguments or intense moments in the future but it didn't matter. They were two people in love and they would deal with everything that popped up.

"I love him," Zach said grinning like a schoolboy, "and that means I'll take the so-called risk,"

Lora frowned. "You can't love him,"

Zach looked at Jayden and he really did love those light blue eyes, they were perfect.

"Why not?" Zach asked. "He's kind, caring and just so great. And honestly, I want to see where this relationship goes, I'm not scared anymore and if you have a problem with that then I don't need you in my life,"

Jayden kissed Zach on the cheek then Zach kissed Jayden on the lips. They might have been kissing for over a week now but Zach still flat out loved how great of a kisser Jayden was. He never ever wanted to stop kissing this beautiful man.

"You know what," Lora said smiling. "If you're happy then I can be happy for you too. I actually haven't liked the past week very much,"

Zach cocked his head. He had spoken to some of

their other friends in his lectures and they had all been spending lots of time with Lora.

"And yes I know I spend a lot of time with the gang at the bar but… they aren't you,"

Zach laughed. "I am pretty great,"

Zach loved hearing Jayden and Lora laugh together and then Zach hugged his best friend.

And for the next three hours, Zach just grinned, laughed and talked with his boyfriend and his best friend for the first time ever. They spoke about their lives, their degrees and everything in-between.

Zach loved every moment of it because it just showed him the power of having honest conversations and standing up for the person he loved.

Now there was only one problem left to deal with and Zach could be with Jayden forever. Something he was definitely looking forward to.

They had to deal with Ryan.

CHAPTER 22
26th February 2024
Canterbury, England

Jayden had never expected to like Lora as much as he did but after spending a few hours with her in the library café, texting her a little and meeting with her and his friends this morning, he couldn't deny that she was actually a great woman with a really interesting life.

But this was the moment they had all been planning for the past two days.

Jayden held Zach's wonderfully soft, smooth hand tight with Lora, Caroline and Jackie close behind them (Katie was already at their destination talking with Ryan to stall him from escaping) as they went through the large brown corridors with gym lockers lining the walls as they went towards the main sports hall.

Jayden couldn't help but grin as he could see that Zach was getting a little turned on because of the slight aroma of sweat that filled the corridor. Maybe Ryan's football team had just finished a practice session and Jayden playfully jabbed his boyfriend.

"Relax I am getting distracted," Zach said, "but I might give you a little reward later,"

Jayden's stomach filled with butterflies at the idea of having sex with the man he loved. He would love that.

They all went through the white doors and then hooked a left and then a right through more gym-locker-lined corridors before they made it to the main sports hall.

Jayden was surprised how massive it was without all the stalls and other students inside. The immense football pitch was all marked out, the block walls of the hall were gigantic and the three other people in the hall looked like ants from this distance.

They all went towards the three people. Jayden could see Katie a mile away with her blue tank-top, short-shorts and black fan that she was still fanning herself with. He was never going to understand her.

Jayden's heart started to pound in his chest. his ears rang slightly. His stomach tightened into a painful knot.

He could see Ryan and Colin talking to Katie. They looked annoyed as hell and Jayden really couldn't have anything bad happen, not today, not any day.

"Babe?" Zach asked. "You alright?"

Jayden kept on walking but he smiled as his body

relaxed. He actually was okay, for the first time since August, maybe ever because he truly was okay. He was with his friends, Lora and his boyfriend.

This was everything he had ever wanted and Jayden couldn't believe how great it felt to have friends and a boyfriend that cared, liked and wanted to be with him. He didn't have to panic or be scared about them leaving him because they had all chosen to be friends with him and they liked him for him, and there was no changing that.

Jackie, Caroline and Katie had proved that time and time again, and Jayden had really liked how they had taught him how healthy friendships worked after a few problems. And they were still here today and wanted to help him.

And Zach was still here and loved him and was an amazing boyfriend because… he just was. Jayden was never going to question that because it didn't need to be questioned. Jayden loved him too.

"That wasn't a foul in the last minute!" Colin shouted at Katie.

"Don't you dare shout at her," Jayden said a lot harsher than he normally would.

"Oh my god the loser and the dumbass are still together. And what?" Ryan asked with a massive grin. "Lora, I thought you were better than that, he lied to you,"

Lora shook her head. "You are nothing but a liar that manipulates people to make them miserable,"

Ryan shrugged like that was nothing.

"I might have loved you once," Zach said, "but I will never love you again. I don't even know what I saw in you,"

Jayden smiled even more as Ryan's grin disappeared. Jayden had no idea that would hurt Ryan, maybe Ryan still loved Zach and was only trying to get him back.

"Come on babe let's go," Colin said. "Let's leave these losers alone,"

Ryan shook his head. "But… but I don't understand how *this* happened?"

Jayden laughed as Ryan shook his head around and highlighted how him and Zach were holding hands like a true couple.

"Because," Jayden said, "you will never understand true love. Love doesn't have to be explained, logical or make that much sense. Love is about respect, joy and that strange feeling you have inside you whenever you see that person,"

Jayden so badly wanted to kiss Zach but he didn't want to go out of his way to annoy Ryan. Jayden was annoyed at him, he didn't want to be cruel to the idiot.

"And Jayden's amazing," Caroline said pulling on her knitted scarf.

Ryan frowned and Jayden was surprised when his shoulders slumped forward and he looked really down.

"Babe come on," Colin said starting to walk away.

Ryan took a step towards Zach and everyone except Colin took two steps closer to Zach. Jayden was not letting Ryan anywhere near his boyfriend.

"We really aren't getting back together are we?"

"No," Zach said. "You were lovely once and I think when you aren't being a dick, you might still be lovely. But no I don't love you anymore and I haven't since August. Since I met Jayden here, what he did to you back then was awful and he triggered so much for you. I get that but you could have handled a lot of stuff differently,"

"We all could have," Lora said.

Jayden felt a lump form in his throat.

"Yeah you're right," Ryan said and he looked at Jayden. "I forgive you and I'm really sorry for what you went through,"

"And you," Jayden said stepping forward and hugging Ryan.

When Jayden broke the hug, Ryan gave Zach a little kiss on the cheek for old time's sake and Jayden just grinned as Ryan and Colin walked away hand in hand.

He wasn't really sure why he was smiling so much, or why his stomach filled with a swarm of butterflies or why he felt so damn amazing. But he had a feeling that it was because everything was settled and perfect. He had a wonderful boyfriend that loved him more than anything, he had so many friends that he really liked and they were so much fun to be around, and Ryan wasn't going to bother them anymore.

That was the great thing about dealing with the past. It could be dealt with, overcome and everyone could move on in the end.

And as Jayden kissed Zach's wonderfully soft, full lips again, he had to admit he was the luckiest man in the world. And he couldn't help but appreciate that he had sorted everything out in the sports hall where him and Zach had reconnected and ultimately started their journey of falling in love.

A journey that had to be the best journey in the world.

CHAPTER 23
24th April 2024
Canterbury, England

About two months later, Zach really enjoyed how warm and light the evenings were starting to get now it was April, and it might have been the Easter Break away from the university, but Zach still loved spending every minute of every day with stunning Jayden.

Over the past three months, they had spent every day together and kissed and done more adult things almost as often. Zach really liked hanging out with Jayden alone with all their friends and he didn't even consider Lora his friend or Caroline, Jackie and Katie Jayden's friends anymore.

They were all their friends and he really liked that.

Zach still didn't want to admit how much he was enjoying photography with Jayden, and he was so damn proud of Jayden for starting to sell photos to magazines, on his own online store and he was making good money from it.

And the past three months were the best ones of his life.

"I love you," Jayden said.

Zach brushed Jayden's smooth hair as they both sat on top of the warm grass hill at the university that overlooked the striking city of Canterbury. There were so many treetops standing up like soldiers but beyond that there were tons of ancient rooftops, the Cathedral spire and so many other landmarks showing off Canterbury's impressive history.

Zach had always loved sitting here in the evenings and talking with his friends and past boyfriends, but this time it felt extra special. Him and Jayden had sat here a few times but tonight, it just seemed extra romantic and Zach couldn't deny he was really enjoying stroking Jayden's hair. It was so smooth and nice that Zach didn't want to stop for a while.

"Don't forget we're meeting your parents tomorrow?" Jayden asked.

Zach laughed. He was looking forward to that a lot more than he wanted to admit, because it would be fun. His parents would pretend to be tough and interrogating because they were somewhat aware of what had happened back in August, but Zach knew after the first ten minutes they would love Jayden.

They would be able to see he was happy, in love and Jayden was so much better than Ryan. Zach was still surprised Ryan and Colin were together and Zach had seen them together a few times since they had sorted out everything, and he had to admit, Ryan and Colin looked even better than they did when they were dating.

"What you thinking about?" Jayden asked.

"Oh, nothing much," Zach said grinning. "Just how you and me are a great couple, how much I love you and how much better my life is now I know you,"

Jayden laughed and blew Zach a kiss. Zach playfully ran a hand down Jayden's hot, sexy body and nodded at a group of girls in summer dresses as they walked past.

Zach moved over a little as Jayden sat up and pulled him close.

"You know why tonight feels even more romantic than normal," Jayden said more of a statement than a question, "and we've known each other a long time to be honest,"

Zach nodded. They might have only been friends and dating for a total of six months including their first attempt in August, but Zach felt like he knew everything about Jayden, and Jayden had said the same about him.

"Yeah, we've been through more together in a few months than most couples ever have to deal with," Zach said smiling.

"Exactly," Jayden said taking a small black box out of his pocket. "Zach James will you do me the honour of becoming my husband?"

"Yes!" Zach shouted kissing, hugging and making the beautiful man he loved fall backwards onto the grass. Then they rolled over kissing and celebrating the best news in their entire lives.

And that was what happened.

They both went to Zach's parent's house the next day and it was the best time of their lives, because Zach's parents were happy, delighted and they were more enthusiastic about the wedding than they were (something Zach had no idea was possible).

Then 9-months later in the Christmas break from university, they married and Zach flat out loved it, because him and the man he loved more than anything in the entire world were together forever. And neither one of them had a problem with that in the slightest.

And Zach realised on his wedding day that when you truly love someone like how Zach loved Jayden and Jayden loved Zach, it didn't matter who they were before, how bad their life was or their mental health, people could improve, get better and life could be great.

Zach was so proud of Jayden for everything he had accomplished and they had both helped each other be better in ways Zach never thought was possible.

And as Zach and Jayden drove off towards the airport for their honeymoon, Zach felt like the luckiest man alive because him and Jayden had gone through damage, healing and love and that made their love even stronger.

Something Zach would always, always treasure.

GET YOUR FREE SHORT STORY NOW! And get signed up to Connor Whiteley's newsletter to hear about new gripping books, offers and exciting projects. (You'll never be sent spam)

https://www.subscribepage.io/gayromancesignup

About the author:

Connor Whiteley is the author of over 60 books in the sci-fi fantasy, nonfiction psychology and books for writer's genre and he is a Human Branding Speaker and Consultant.

He is a passionate warhammer 40,000 reader, psychology student and author.

Who narrates his own audiobooks and he hosts The Psychology World Podcast.

All whilst studying Psychology at the University of Kent, England.

Also, he was a former Explorer Scout where he gave a speech to the Maltese President in August 2018 and he attended Prince Charles' 70th Birthday Party at Buckingham Palace in May 2018.

Plus, he is a self-confessed coffee lover!

Other books by Connor Whiteley:

Bettie English Private Eye Series
A Very Private Woman
The Russian Case

A Very Urgent Matter
A Case Most Personal
Trains, Scots and Private Eyes
The Federation Protects
Cops, Robbers and Private Eyes
Just Ask Bettie English
An Inheritance To Die For
The Death of Graham Adams
Bearing Witness
The Twelve
The Wrong Body
The Assassination Of Bettie English
Wining And Dying
Eight Hours
Uniformed Cabal
A Case Most Christmas

<u>Gay Romance Novellas</u>
Breaking, Nursing, Repairing A Broken Heart
Jacob And Daniel
Fallen For A Lie
Spying And Weddings
Clean Break
Awakening Love
Meeting A Country Man
Loving Prime Minister
Snowed In Love
Never Been Kissed
Love Betrays You

Lord of War Origin Trilogy:
Not Scared Of The Dark
Madness
Burn Them All

Way Of The Odyssey
Odyssey of Rebirth
Convergence of Odysseys

The Fireheart Fantasy Series
Heart of Fire
Heart of Lies
Heart of Prophecy
Heart of Bones
Heart of Fate

City of Assassins (Urban Fantasy)
City of Death
City of Martyrs
City of Pleasure
City of Power

Agents of The Emperor
Return of The Ancient Ones
Vigilance
Angels of Fire
Kingmaker
The Eight
The Lost Generation
Hunt

GAY ROMANCE COLLECTION VOLUME 4

Emperor's Council
Speaker of Treachery
Birth Of The Empire
Terraforma
Spaceguard

The Rising Augusta Fantasy Adventure Series
Rise To Power
Rising Walls
Rising Force
Rising Realm

Lord Of War Trilogy (Agents of The Emperor)
Not Scared Of The Dark
Madness
Burn It All Down

Miscellaneous:
RETURN
FREEDOM
SALVATION
Reflection of Mount Flame
The Masked One
The Great Deer
English Independence

OTHER SHORT STORIES BY CONNOR WHITELEY
Mystery Short Story Collections

Criminally Good Stories Volume 1: 20 Detective Mystery Short Stories
Criminally Good Stories Volume 2: 20 Private Investigator Short Stories
Criminally Good Stories Volume 3: 20 Crime Fiction Short Stories
Criminally Good Stories Volume 4: 20 Science Fiction and Fantasy Mystery Short Stories
Criminally Good Stories Volume 5: 20 Romantic Suspense Short Stories

Connor Whiteley Starter Collections:
Agents of The Emperor Starter Collection
Bettie English Starter Collection
Matilda Plum Starter Collection
Gay Romance Starter Collection
Way Of The Odyssey Starter Collection
Kendra Detective Fiction Starter Collection

Mystery Short Stories:
Protecting The Woman She Hated
Finding A Royal Friend
Our Woman In Paris
Corrupt Driving
A Prime Assassination
Jubilee Thief
Jubilee, Terror, Celebrations
Negative Jubilation
Ghostly Jubilation

Killing For Womenkind
A Snowy Death
Miracle Of Death
A Spy In Rome
The 12:30 To St Pancreas
A Country In Trouble
A Smokey Way To Go
A Spicy Way To GO
A Marketing Way To Go
A Missing Way To Go
A Showering Way To Go
Poison In The Candy Cane
Kendra Detective Mystery Collection Volume 1
Kendra Detective Mystery Collection Volume 2
Mystery Short Story Collection Volume 1
Mystery Short Story Collection Volume 2
Criminal Performance
Candy Detectives
Key To Birth In The Past

Science Fiction Short Stories:
Their Brave New World
Gummy Bear Detective
The Candy Detective
What Candies Fear
The Blurred Image
Shattered Legions
The First Rememberer
Life of A Rememberer
System of Wonder

Lifesaver
Remarkable Way She Died
The Interrogation of Annabella Stormic
Blade of The Emperor
Arbiter's Truth
Computation of Battle
Old One's Wrath
Puppets and Masters
Ship of Plague
Interrogation
Edge of Failure

<u>Fantasy Short Stories:</u>
City of Snow
City of Light
City of Vengeance
Dragons, Goats and Kingdom
Smog The Pathetic Dragon
Don't Go In The Shed
The Tomato Saver
The Remarkable Way She Died
Dragon Coins
Dragon Tea
Dragon Rider

All books in 'An Introductory Series':
Clinical Psychology and Transgender Clients
Clinical Psychology
Careers In Psychology
Psychology of Suicide
Dementia Psychology
Clinical Psychology Reflections Volume 4
Forensic Psychology of Terrorism And Hostage-Taking
Forensic Psychology of False Allegations
Year In Psychology
CBT For Anxiety
CBT For Depression
Applied Psychology
BIOLOGICAL PSYCHOLOGY 3RD EDITION
COGNITIVE PSYCHOLOGY THIRD EDITION
SOCIAL PSYCHOLOGY- 3RD EDITION
ABNORMAL PSYCHOLOGY 3RD EDITION
PSYCHOLOGY OF RELATIONSHIPS- 3RD EDITION
DEVELOPMENTAL PSYCHOLOGY 3RD EDITION
HEALTH PSYCHOLOGY
RESEARCH IN PSYCHOLOGY
A GUIDE TO MENTAL HEALTH AND TREATMENT AROUND THE WORLD- A GLOBAL LOOK AT DEPRESSION
FORENSIC PSYCHOLOGY
THE FORENSIC PSYCHOLOGY OF THEFT,

BURGLARY AND OTHER CRIMES AGAINST PROPERTY
CRIMINAL PROFILING: A FORENSIC PSYCHOLOGY GUIDE TO FBI PROFILING AND GEOGRAPHICAL AND STATISTICAL PROFILING.
CLINICAL PSYCHOLOGY
FORMULATION IN PSYCHOTHERAPY
PERSONALITY PSYCHOLOGY AND INDIVIDUAL DIFFERENCES
CLINICAL PSYCHOLOGY REFLECTIONS VOLUME 2
Clinical Psychology Reflections Volume 3
CULT PSYCHOLOGY
Police Psychology

A Psychology Student's Guide To University
How Does University Work?
A Student's Guide To University And Learning
University Mental Health and Mindset